# He remembered the first time he saw Tamarind back in June....

With her toned arms, she'd flipped the brisket on the grill as if it were nothing then caught him staring at her. Just like he was doing again now.

"So, *you're* the one they were talking about at the chamber of commerce meeting." The terse statement explained her glare.

"I was going to shoot you an e-mail, or call...."

"That would have been nice, you know."

"You didn't miss me at all?" He tried to smile away her aggravation. "I'm on your side, really."

"Looks like you're sampling my menu, is what you're doing. Only two people know the secret of my sauce, that's me and my dad. I'll never tell you." Tamarind glanced at the plates arrayed in front of him.

"The pork is amazing." He reached for a rib and took a bite. This sauce was different than the pork. Chipotle peppers, definitely.

"Flattery won't change the fact that you're the one opening a barbecu⬛⬛⬛⬛⬛⬛⬛⬛⬛⬛⬛ place. You went th⬛⬛⬛⬛⬛⬛⬛⬛⬛⬛⬛⬛⬛ Tamarind bit her l⬛⬛⬛⬛⬛⬛⬛⬛⬛⬛⬛

## LYNETTE SOWELL

is an award-winning author with New England roots, but she makes her home in central Texas with her husband and a herd of five cats. When she's not writing, she edits medical reports and chases down stories for the local newspaper. You can find out more about Lynette at lynettesowell.com, or find her on Facebook.

Books by Lynette Sowell

## HEARTSONG PRESENTS

HP863—*All That Glitters*
HP970—*Catch a Falling Star*
HP990—*Counting on Starlight*

# The Sweetheart of Starlight

*Lynette Sowell*

Heartsong Presents

He determines the number of the stars
and calls them each by name.
*Psalms* 147:4

This is dedicated to my sweet husband, who always pushes me
to go that extra mile on those days when I'm not sure if I can.
Everyone should have an encourager like you in their lives!

This is also dedicated to my dear friends who are like family in
the Fort Hood area. From all around the world, we've found our ways
here together. My life is enriched because of people like you.

A note from the Author:

*I love to hear from my readers! You may correspond with me by
writing:*

**Lynette Sowell
Author Relations
P.O. Box 9048
Buffalo, NY 14240-9048**

**ISBN-13: 978-0-373-48625-0**

**THE SWEETHEART OF STARLIGHT**

This edition issued by special arrangement with Barbour Publishing,
Inc., 1810 Barbour Drive, Uhrichsville, Ohio, U.S.A.

Copyright © 2012 by Lynette Sowell

Scripture taken from the HOLY BIBLE, NEW INTERNATIONAL VERSION®.
NIV®. Copyright © 1973, 1978, 1984, 2011 by Biblica, Inc.™ Used by
permission. All rights reserved worldwide.

This is a work of fiction. Names, characters, places and incidents are
either the product of the author's imagination or are used fictitiously,
and any resemblance to actual persons, living or dead, business
establishments, events or locales is entirely coincidental.

® and ™ are trademarks of the publisher. Trademarks indicated with ®
are registered in the United States Patent and Trademark Office, the
Canadian Trade Marks Office and in other countries.

PRINTED IN THE U.S.A.

# *Prologue*

*August, Oklahoma City*

Tamarind Brown could barely lift the trophy in all its electroplated glory, but she grinned anyway as digital cameras clicked and flashed in her direction. Sweat snaked a fresh trail down her back and along her temples. She surveyed the cheering crowd and allowed herself a moment under the great shining sun. *That's right.* The title is *mine. Mine!* If only Daddy had come to see this one. Three days, sweating over the smoker. Trying not to worry, praying as she coaxed tendrils of smoke from the applewood to infuse the meat roasting on the rack above.

"Congratulations, Ms. Brown." The emcee of the Great Southwest Barbecue Extravaganza handed her an envelope. Tamarind already knew the check amount inside. Enough for gas money home, and then some.

"Thanks, Bud." She smiled at him as she shifted the ginormous trophy to her hip. Bud winked at her before she scanned the crowd again. *Sorry, Bud, you're old enough to be my dad.*

Another smiling face in the crowd, though, made her pause. Rick Mantovani, grinning at her with those snappy dark eyes of his and applauding. He gave her a nod then whistled through his fingers. Sure, he'd won in the pulled pork category, placed second in chicken. They'd chased each other throughout the Southwest this summer from one barbecue competition to the next. But no, she'd won the overall title with her beef barbecue points. She gave him a nod, complete with plenty of her own personal sauce.

Then the crowd swarmed after Bud declared the competition over, and Tamarind lost sight of Rick's Cheshire cat expression. He would probably hop the next flight back to New York. That thought alone almost made her quit smiling…just a little. Wasn't he going to tell her good-bye, at least? He mentioned something about shooting her an e-mail after they both returned to their respective homes, his in northern New Jersey and hers in central Texas.

Right. They both ran restaurants and had stolen the time this summer to sneak off to try their hands at competitive barbecue. Most likely she'd never see him again.

Tamarind made herself keep smiling. As some of her fellow competitors congratulated her, the sound of their voices garbled together, reminding Tamarind of the sound of the lunch crowd back at The Pit in Starlight. Home.

# *Chapter 1*

Texas in February wasn't supposed to be this cold.

Rick shivered as he crossed the parking lot, dodging the occasional puddle as he did so. The wind's icy breath pressed on his coat and whipped the Texas flag that flew from the flagpole near the restaurant's entrance. A wisp of smoke rose behind the building. The scent of mesquite drifted in his direction.

He paused before going inside and glanced at the assortment of pickup trucks in the parking lot. Tamarind would probably flip if she knew he was here and that he didn't tell her he was coming. It was easier this way, his explanation kept for the right time. Not on the phone, or e-mail. In person.

She had a nice place. A carefully screen-printed sign in lettering that looked much like brown logs tied together with rope to form the letters, The Pit, with a subtitle in flowing script: Barbecue and More. The script was a little bit of sass along with the rustic words. The contrast made him smile.

Rick pulled open the glass door, which stuck a little. The last of the breakfast aromas inside struck him—ham, eggs, toast, with the unmistakable underlying notes of freshly brewed coffee.

The other diners looked up. Rick nodded an apology for the swirl of cold air that followed him inside. The main dining area was a combination of the typical vinyl booths at the perimeter of the room with blocks of tables filling the center.

Too bad Tamarind's prize money wasn't enough to replace her old cushioned, vinyl-upholstered booths. Rick knew the pressure of keeping costs down and customers coming into the restaurant. His restaurants might be nearly sixteen hundred miles away, but he faced the same obstacles. Yet business was good for him, even in the tough economy.

"Seat yourself wherever you can find a spot," called out a cheerful server from where she stood at the cash register, not ten paces away.

"Thanks." He ignored the curious looks and found a spot in a corner booth. As he sat down, he ran his right hand across the surface of the table. Clean. His stomach rumbled. *Patience. You'll be full soon enough...and then some.* He looked at his phone before setting it on the table. Just after eleven. Early enough to get some lunch. Or brunch, if he wanted to get technical about it.

Rick pulled a menu from the holder. The front displayed the same logo from the sign outside. He was tempted to order breakfast, but he really wanted to get to the barbecue.

"Coffee?" The pert server, her name tag reading Suzie, wore a simple navy-blue polo shirt over black pants.

"Yes, please. Ice water, too."

"Do you know what you'd like to order?"

He smiled at the twang in her voice. "I need a few minutes."

"Sure enough. I'll be right back." She turned on her heel and sashayed off.

Rick looked back down at the menu in simple black and white. He'd start with the pork barbecue sandwich, Kansas City style—or so the menu proclaimed. "Cleo's special recipe," it also said. A side order of sweet potato fries would go nicely, at a dollar more instead of regular steak fries—hand cut.

Suzie returned with his coffee in a simple brown ceramic mug, the ice water in an opaque plastic glass. "You decided?"

"The Kansas City pork barbecue sandwich and a side of sweet potato fries, to start."

She wrote it down. "To start, huh?"

"I brought my appetite." He smiled at her.

She giggled. "Good thing. This place is the best. I'll go put this right in." Off she went toward the kitchen, pulling a ticket off her order pad.

So Tamarind's place wasn't electronic. Not a good way to track costs and sales history. She'd have to be extra careful with her budget. Not having a good tracking system could cost her thousands. If things went well between them, maybe he'd convince her to upgrade. That's if things went well, of course. Rick took a sip of the coffee. Not bad.

He studied the dining room, and his gaze connected with an older woman at a booth diagonally across the room from him. Her red hair was blown into a style his mother would love. Lydia Mantovani had hers set and styled every week and was probably about this lady's age. The redhead's eyes narrowed ever so slightly. Then she glanced at the older, balding gentleman sitting across from her and started talking.

Tamarind had told him once that where she lived in Texas was different than most Texas towns. Close to the Fort Hood military base, Starlight and its neighboring towns drew people from all over the world. They were used to strangers. So what was with this lady's expression, if that was true?

Never mind. He opened his notepad and starting making notes about the menu. For one thing, Tamarind had thirty—no, thirty-five—lunch and supper items. Rick forced himself to quit thinking about ways to "fix" Tamarind's restaurant and on his own reasons for being here. He looked at his phone. Ten minutes now since the server had left with his order. A couple entered the restaurant and did as he'd done a few moments ago, scanning the room for a free spot.

At least three tables had been vacated since he'd entered, and they still held plates, silverware, cups, and soiled napkins. His server emerged from another area of the restaurant, lugging a gray plastic tub. She started clearing the closest table.

Rick took that to mean his meal wasn't up yet. He studied the well-used vinyl booths, the sturdy yet old tile floor. The walls were a cheerful shade of terra-cotta.

Prints from the Texas countryside alternated with vintage kitchen utensils on the walls.

His server disappeared with the full bucket of dishes after wiping down the now-empty tables. Rick glanced across the dining room again. The redhead was eyeballing him again. This time, the man sharing her booth glanced in his direction.

Did they know him? He couldn't imagine how.

Here came the server, carrying a simple melamine plate that held Rick's sandwich and fries. "Sorry about the wait. We're a little shorthanded this morning." She set the plate in front of him and placed the paper ticket facedown at the edge of the table.

"No problem." Rick's mouth watered as he inhaled the aroma rising from the fresh pulled-pork sandwich.

"Need any hot sauce?"

He shook his head. "This is fine. But hold on. While I've got you here, I'd like half an order of your baby back ribs, a quarter-pound of your slow-smoked beef brisket."

Her eyes widened, and she started a new ticket. "All righty." She left him to take his first bite.

Rick opened his mouth and chomped down on the pork sandwich. Tender, meaty. The pork's texture was soft enough that it melted, but not mushy. He let the spices and sauce slide across his palate. Tangy, with a little heat. Cleo's specialty, huh? That would be Tamarind's dad, a towering wall of an African American with graying hair and a booming voice that reminded Rick of the actor Michael Clark Duncan. He'd met Cleo Brown, once. Tried not to squirm like a kid when they'd shaken hands at a barbecue competition somewhere in East Texas.

He should have ordered all this food to go so he could sample and taste and take notes in the privacy of his own duplex apartment. He could have sworn there was cinnamon in the sauce. Or was that pungent spice cloves instead? Rick wrote *Cloves?* on his notepad.

"Thirty-five degrees out, and they're still coming for lunch. Good news for us." Tamarind snatched a new order ticket from the pass-through. "Mike—I need a chef salad and a turkey salad sandwich, two sides chicken soup!"

Suzie sauntered up to the window. "Got another order from fourteen." She grinned.

"What do you mean, another order? Didn't we just send an order out to fourteen?"

"Yup. But that cute guy must have a big honkin' appetite."

"Who is it?"

"No idea." She shrugged. "But I'd definitely recognize him if I saw him again. I love that dark wavy hair. And those eyes…"

Tamarind slid the ticket from the stainless-steel shelf. "Half a rack of ribs, plus the beef…after pulled pork and a side of sweet tater fries?" Suzie wasn't kidding when she mentioned a big, honkin' appetite.

"As long as he pays his bill, he can sit there all day and pig out, and I won't care." No sides or salads or cold sandwiches, so she'd see to this ticket herself. She pulled the pan of brisket out of the warmer, fresh from smoking overnight. A few slices short of the full order, so she took up the carving knife. It was best served freshly cut, anyway. Her hand slipped, and the blade bounced off her index finger.

She dropped the knife on the board, yanking her finger away from the meat. A clean line bloomed red on her finger. The pain made her blink. "Mike—finish this for me—I've got a cut."

"No prob, Tams." Mike was at her side in a flash. "Take all the time you need."

"Ha. Won't need much." Tamarind hurried to the first-aid kit near the office door. She didn't mind the breather. There was nothing in the world like working at a job you loved, but this morning her feet hurt already, and her brain hurt, too, thinking of the end of the month drawing nearer. She'd make payroll, but then the electric bill was out the wazoo with the recent cold snap. Tamarind sighed. Something had to change, and fast. Her parents hadn't put up so much money to finance the down payment for her dream, for her to let them down.

The discussion from last night's Starlight Chamber of Commerce meeting echoed in her ears. Several new businesses were on the horizon for their town. Development would bring jobs, more customers. Good news for Starlight. There was some rumbling about a new restaurant coming, possibly, as the city council had approved a zoning change from residential to commercial at the old Millicent home on Main Street.

*"I hear it's some big shot from the Northeast, thinks he can come down here and do barbecue."*

Tamarind wanted to cry at that news. She'd lain awake until long past 2 a.m. *God, this was no surprise to You, but I wish You'd let me in on the news.* No answers had been forthcoming before she drifted off to sleep and dreamed about an empty restaurant.

Someone had left an empty Band-Aid box in the first-aid kit, Tamarind discovered as she rummaged through its contents. With another sigh, she took herself back to the office. There were a few Band-Aids in her top desk drawer. She ignored the stack of bills on the desk. They'd be waiting for her tonight.

She wrapped her cut finger with a bandage. The cut was still bleeding. She couldn't go back on the line like this. Mike had been squirming like a kid on the last day of school to run the line himself. Well, he'd get his chance. If she had to wait tables and run the register, she'd do it. She'd done it before.

Tamarind headed back to the line. "Mike, this cut's not stopping yet. Can you take over for me for a few?" She had the feeling that Suzie was in the weeds out front and not saying anything.

"Of course I can. You go on out front." He shot a smile at her, a brilliant white on his face.

The look made her pause for an instant. Then her stomach flopped. Mike's smile lent an extra few degrees to the warm kitchen. Tamarind hurried to the dining room. Maybe she'd imagined it. Maybe she was looking for something that wasn't even there. *Right...definitely not with Mike.*

Tamarind grabbed the nearest empty bus tub. If she were looking for someone, it wouldn't be Mike. He was, well—just Mike. Faithful employee. A friend. He'd listened when her heart had shattered like a plate hitting the floor almost two years ago when Billy Tucker had fallen for Justine Campbell. She healed and moved on.

She stopped at Azalea and Herb Bush's booth. "G'morning. Y'all are brave for coming out on such a cold day."

"Well, I wasn't up to cooking this morning, and Herb was pitchin' a fit for something 'meaty,' so of course we had to come out." Azalea's red hair looked like she'd had a fresh color touch up. She patted it gently. "Though that wind out there like to have blown us down the street with the truck engine not even running."

"We're due for an ice storm," said Herb. "You'd better believe it." He rubbed his hands together then rubbed calloused fingers on his tattooed forearms.

"Don't you two even *think* about coming out when it gets that bad." Tamarind laid her free hand on Azalea's shoulder. The older woman was like an aunt to her and others in Starlight. The idea of anything happening to either one of them...

"Don't worry about us. We've got the sense to stay in if it's really bad." Azalea waved as if trying to brush away Tamarind's concern.

"I know. But I also know how stubborn you are," Tamarind said with a smile. "Do y'all need a refill on coffee? I can get it after I bus this table."

"No, we're fine. But that fine young fella in the corner staring at us looks like he needs more ice water." Azalea shook her head. "Ice water. And it's near freezing outside."

Tamarind glanced at the corner booth and froze. *Rick, in Starlight?*

## Chapter 2

As soon as Tamarind looked in his direction, Rick wanted to sink deeper into the vinyl cushion, if that were possible. Her face flickered with a combination of shock, then…irritation?

She said something to the older couple, and the red-haired woman nodded as if she knew *exactly* what Tamarind meant. Tamarind stepped to the next booth and started clearing the table, turning her back on Rick and leaving him to stare at his half-eaten pork sandwich.

As his older brother and sister used to tease him years ago when he'd get in trouble: *"Ricky, you've got a lot of 'splaining to do."* He should have kept in touch with Tamarind since the summer. But he was busy. She had to understand that, running a restaurant herself. Restaurants were a sixty-hour-per-week job, often more. Still, the memory of her laugh, her smile, her wit should have been enough to make him call, or e-mail at least.

He watched Tamarind lug the bus tub back toward the kitchen area. Yes, he should have called, warned her, or something. No wonder he hadn't had a date in, well... He couldn't remember.

Donny and Graciela had found spouses and started providing his mother with grandchildren, so she left Rick alone about his unattached status, except for holiday and family birthday dinners. If anything, he was married to both *Mantovani's* and *Pasta-Pasta*.

"Your ribs and brisket, sir." Tamarind stood at the table, setting both plates down with a clunk. She glanced over her shoulder then slid onto the cushion across from him and squinted with those wide green eyes of hers.

He remembered the first time he saw Tamarind back in June, as she hovered over a smoker, her wild dark hair pulled back with a red bandanna, beads of perspiration on her forehead. With her toned arms, she'd flipped the brisket on the grill as if it were nothing then caught him staring at her. Just like he was doing again now.

"So, *you're* the one they were talking about at the chamber of commerce meeting." The terse statement explained her glare.

"I was going to shoot you an e-mail, or call...."

"That would have been nice, you know."

"You didn't miss me at all?" He tried to smile away her aggravation. "I'm on your side, really."

"Looks like you're sampling my menu, is what you're doing. Only two people know the secret of my sauce, that's me and my dad. I'll never tell you." Tamarind glanced at the plates arrayed in front of him.

"The pork is amazing." He reached for a rib and took

a bite. This sauce was different than the pork. Chipotle peppers, definitely.

"Flattery won't change the fact that you're the one opening a barbecue restaurant in the old Millicent place. You went through rezoning and everything." Tamarind bit her lip. "And you didn't tell me."

"I probably should have. I wasn't sure if it was going to go through, for one thing. That Starlight City Council's a tough bunch. But the property is perfect for what I have in mind, and the lot is large enough to put in a good parking lot." Rick realized the volume of his voice had risen, but then Tamarind's own tone had caused a few of the diners to look their way.

"But why here? Why not in New York? Don't they eat barbecue there?" The question hung between them.

A crash from the kitchen made him flinch. Tamarind looked over her shoulder. "Don't answer that just yet. I need to run."

"I'll be here." Rick felt like a heel as Tamarind hurried back to the kitchen.

The older couple had risen and were now zigzagging between tables in his direction. The redheaded lady was mumbling something to her husband, who shot her a stern look as he approached. He extended his hand toward Rick, who stood and wiped his hands on a napkin.

"Herb Bush," the man said as they shook, his firm grip surprising Rick.

"Rick Mantovani."

"So you're the fella that Tamarind has talked about ever since getting home again from that last barbecue competition." Herb studied Rick as if regarding a new employee.

"She mentioned me?" Now this was interesting. He really did feel sorry he hadn't called or written.

"Don't get too high 'n' mighty feeling, young man," said the redheaded woman. "From what it sounds like to me, you had a good friendship started, and now, after all this time—"

Herb shot his wife a look that silenced her. "So you're going to open a barbecue place at the old Millicent house?"

"Early spring. We just closed on the building this week, and it'll take a couple of months to get the renovations completed."

"No wonder Tamarind's got a fire lit under her, and it's barely above freezing outside." Azalea shook her head.

"This is nothing personal. It's just business. I've looked at the numbers, and the central Texas economy is one of the fastest growing in the country. Sometime back, I received a brochure highlighting Starlight's business outlook for restaurateurs. So I decided to start here with the first in a new series of restaurants—upscale, down-home style. If anything, Tamarind helped seal the deal for me. The way she talked about her town, it convinced me that Starlight is a great place to open a business. I'm going to hire at least half a dozen workers." Why did he sound like he was making excuses?

Azalea grunted. "But *Tamarind* sells the barbecue here in Starlight. Everyone knows that."

"A little healthy competition will be good for The Pit. People want variety." Rick glanced around the dining room. "People will learn to appreciate her food even more. I want to help her. Plus, there are plenty of people in Starlight, plus people from the little towns out west who'll come here."

"Now, calm down, son." Herb held up his right hand. "Zalea here is just a little protective of our girl. Time will tell if you're like some of the others that have come here before. They're happy to buy buildings, start businesses, and then skedaddle if things don't go their way. Then we're left with an empty building and no one working to fill it."

"I'm not a quitter, Mr. Bush. I already own two thriving restaurants in New York. I've wanted to open a third. After last summer, I knew the time was right to start investigating a site for my new place...my new barbecue place."

"Here in Starlight."

"Yes, here. Matter of fact, I'll make sure you two get an invitation to the grand opening."

"Thank you. We'll be watching to see how things go for you."

The older woman opened her mouth, but Herb took her by the arm. "We'll be seeing you."

Rick nodded then waved toward his server. He figured now was as good a time as any to leave. She approached. "I need my ticket, plus boxes for the food, please."

He made a mental note. From now on, he'd call ahead and pick up his food to go. There was Tamarind zipping through the dining room to another room, probably an extension of the dining room. This definitely wasn't the reunion he'd expected with Tamarind. But there would be plenty of time to patch things up between them and smooth over whatever hard feelings she had.

\* \* \*

"So, how'd you know you wanted to be a cook?" asked a freckle-faced boy in the front row of the auditorium.

Tamarind paused and tried not to rub her sore finger. It probably needed stitches, but she'd nearly forgotten about volunteering to speak at Career Day for the freshmen at Starlight High. She glimpsed her friend, Liann Tucker, at the back of Hattie Hempstead Auditorium.

"I didn't, actually. After I graduated from Starlight High ten years ago, I wasn't sure what I wanted to do. So, I got a job at The Pit and then started taking a few classes over at Central Texas College." She probably sounded like an ad, but that didn't matter. "My dad's the one who's the cook in our family—well, he does barbecue. My mother's German, so she cooks what she knows, and he cooks what he knows."

She glanced toward the moderator of the career panel.

"Any more questions?" asked the guidance counselor. "We have a great opportunity for all of you students to ask questions from a police officer, lawyer, an HVAC worker, an IT specialist, and a cook."

Tamarind kept a smile on her face at the sound of the word *cook*. She wasn't a cook. She was a culinary artist. She found flavors for barbecue that no one else had. People would often drive an hour to eat one of her meals. She raised her hand. "I thought of something else."

The guidance counselor passed her the microphone.

"Not only did I study culinary arts, I studied business management. It's important to know how to run a business if you want it to be successful. I have six employees who depend on me, six families who are affected by how The Pit does." The idea, spoken out loud, made her throat constrict just a little. "But I love what I do. That's important. You need to find what you're passionate about and study that."

"Cheerleaders!" someone shouted, and a few laughs echoed in the room.

The counselor shot a glare in the direction of the mouthy student then glanced at Tamarind. "Thank you, Ms. Brown. And thank you to all of our guests for the career panel. Let's thank them, freshmen."

The audience applauded as Tamarind and the rest of the volunteers stood. Maybe she shouldn't have said anything. But she wasn't just a cook, and people *did* depend on her. The stack of bills lying on her desk reminded her that she needed to stay afloat.

Rick's face drifted into view in her mind's eye. Rick, sitting in a booth at The Pit, sizing up her restaurant as competition. It was one thing for her to compete against him in a barbecue contest, quite another for two businesses to go head-to-head. He had more money, more experience.

Tamarind filed off the stage with the other career experts. Liann was waiting at the end of an aisle for her.

"Hey, you!" Liann gave her a wide grin. "You did great up there."

"Thanks." She trudged along the carpeted ramp that led from the auditorium and into the foyer. Students swirled past them in a current, on the way back to class.

"You don't look very excited about career day." Liann nodded to a young woman passing by.

"See ya in class, Mrs. Tucker!" the student called out.

"It's not that career day is unexciting." Tamarind shrugged. "You'll never guess who's in town."

"That cute chef from New York?" Liann stood to the side. "Move over here. The hallway gets a little cramped at times like this."

Tamarind knew this quite well. Had she ever giggled and squealed like a lot of these girls did, talking and laughing as they went to class? Probably. She had a vague memory of a detention or two for excess talking.

"It's true…. I saw him this morning."

"He *is* here?" Liann clamped her hand over her mouth. "I was only joking."

"Joke all you want, but yes, the very good-looking Rick Mantovani is here, in Starlight. For a good long while, probably."

"I thought he didn't call you or anything after the summer."

"Nope. He's not here for me. He's here for business. And The Pit, well, it's getting by, but barely." Tamarind hated giving voice to her fears. Dad always said never to let listening ears "hear her fear."

"Well, girl. We'll have to fix that. Cute chef or not, we'll figure something out." Liann gave her a hug.

"But you're busy…."

"Aren't we all? But you're my friend, and friends help watch out for each other." A mischievous look entered Liann's eye. "We'll show that Rick what's-his-name how Texans do barbecue."

# Chapter 3

Rick rolled up the contractor's plans and turned off the lights to the old Millicent place. He headed for his rental car. The large, sprawling house's name made him smile. He was literally the new kid in town, but he was already referring to the building as the locals did.

The contractor came highly recommended by a friend who ran a restaurant in Austin. After demolition on the inside of the structure, the renovation would take eight weeks. Then at the height of spring in Texas, he'd celebrate the grand opening of Rick's Texas Barbecue. The details made his head spin. His phone buzzed. *Mom.* He'd promised to call her last night.

"Hey, Ma."

"Ricky, you didn't call." Her voice echoed from the phone. "Your father and I waited up."

"I know, I'm sorry. I was working on restaurant plans. Then when I remembered, I also remembered the time difference." He shivered as the wind sliced into his jacket. He fumbled for the keys with his free hand.

"Texas. You've gone all the way to Texas."

"I know. But it's going to be a great restaurant, Ma. You should see this town. You'd love it."

"Maybe I'll come for the grand opening, if I can get your father on a plane, that is."

"That would be great."

A vehicle on Main Street slowed down then pulled into the driveway and stopped behind his car. *Tamarind?*

"You still there?" his mother asked.

"Yes. I'm at the restaurant now.... A friend of mine just pulled up."

"Well, I'll let you go. Just don't forget to call your mother."

"Of course not. I love ya, Ma."

"You too, Ricky."

They ended the call. It used to drive him nuts when she called him Ricky, but he never told her to stop. Here came Tamarind, before he could make a getaway. Much as he liked seeing her, he wasn't up to any more verbal sparring. Not when he had a night's worth of work ahead of him.

"Hey!" she called out as she left her car.

"Hey yourself. We're not open yet, you know." He couldn't resist teasing her, just a little.

"Uh-huh." A grin split her face. "I heard you think you can make barbecue." She stopped beside the driver's door of his car and crossed her arms across her chest.

"I don't just think. I *know*." Rick smiled back. "Look—about earlier…"

Tamarind shook her head. "No, I'm sorry. I should be flattered that you're trying my food. I just never expected you to show up here, of all places. I never imagined you'd come here."

"Until last summer, neither did I." He could stand here forever, let the wind whistle in his ears, and watch Tamarind's smile along with the myriad of emotions that crossed her face.

"Honestly, Rick, business has been tough this winter." She raised her hands. "Food costs are killing me. Something's got to change, but I don't know how or what. I'll share my resources with you, but it's tough. But then you know that, running restaurants yourself."

No wonder her hackles had shot up, seeing him here in Starlight. Like any restaurant owner, she didn't want to see customers drifting down the street to a competitor.

"Tamarind, I'm not here to put you out of business." He stepped closer. "What's wrong with your finger?"

"Cut it a while ago."

"Well, it's seeping through." He reached for her hand, with the Band-aid-covered index finger. "You probably need stitches."

"I—I'll be okay."

Her hand felt soft and warm. The softness surprised him, especially from someone who worked in a kitchen. She probably used some kind of fancy lotion on it. He swallowed hard. "If you were one of my employees, I'd send you to the doctor."

She gently pulled her hand back. "If it doesn't stay together, I'll go tomorrow and get a butterfly patch on it, or something."

"You'd better." He knew how hard it was to work with a hand injury, but he also knew she'd be stubborn enough to do it, even with pain. "Hey, I'd show you the inside, but there's not much to look at. And I think there's a dead mouse in one of the walls, so it stinks pretty bad."

"I don't have to see it yet." Tamarind stuffed her wounded hand back into her jacket pocket. "I was just passing by and saw a car here. Figured it might be you, so I wanted to apologize for being a snip earlier."

"Don't worry about it. You were working, and I should have told you I was coming to town. You're a better friend than that." He took a step closer and touched her arm.

She smiled and looked him in the eye. He liked how tall she was, that she didn't try to hide her height. "I'm glad you think so. Starlight is a good place to start a business. You're not from around here, but no one will hold that against you. Lots of people pass through here because of the military. So what's one more new person? You just need to show up, make good food, and show that you care. That's all people ask."

Rick opened his mouth to ask her to dinner but stopped. He wasn't planning on making Starlight a permanent place to live. Sure, he planned to be here constantly for at least six months, getting the restaurant up and running, but then once his manager was in place and had the routine down, he'd be back in New York.

"I guess I'll see you around, then," was all he could manage.

Something, he couldn't tell what, flickered in Tamarind's eyes. "Sure. Well, I need to get back. I left The Pit long enough to speak at a career day panel at the high school, but we've got dinner prep to start." She stepped back toward her vehicle. "See you."

Rick unlocked his car then watched as Tamarind backed onto Main Street. He felt as though he'd flubbed somehow, again. It was one thing when they saw each other throughout the summer at competitions on the road, another thing in everyday life. Everyday life didn't hold much time for relationships, even friends. If they weren't related to business, Rick didn't have much to do with other people.

But he wanted to spend more time with Tamarind. He knew she was religious. Maybe church would help him with business, and with Tamarind.

Tamarind's finger throbbed as she turned the key in the lock to her parents' front door. The tingle she'd felt when Rick took her hand almost masked the pain. Why him, why here in Starlight? She needed to quit asking herself and start concentrating on discovering why The Pit was losing money.

If only she could afford one of those computerized systems that logged in the food and kept track of how many dishes she sold each day and each week. She stepped onto the tiled entryway and let the storm door snap shut before turning and closing the main door. She felt sixty-eight tonight, not twenty-eight, and tried not to echo the sigh of the wind outside.

"That you, *Schatze*?" Her mother's voice drifted from the direction of the kitchen.

"It's me." Tamarind kicked off her shoes and inhaled. Mom had made schnitzel tonight, but Tamarind's taste buds were as tired as her feet. Her stomach growled, however. She fluffed her hair with her uninjured hand as she crossed the entry hall and stepped into the kitchen.

Her mother clicked her tongue as Tamarind entered and put her restaurant file on the dining table. "You look exhausted. I'll make you a plate. I've kept everything warm on the stove."

"Not too much. I'm more thirsty than anything at the moment." Tamarind went to the fridge for the iced tea, in spite of the chilly evening.

"You work too hard." Mom reached for a plate in the cabinet. "You should take a break."

"I don't need a break, not really. Besides, tonight will be break enough. Mike's opening in the morning. I told him he could start breakfast, and I'll come in at ten." She took a swallow of the tea she'd poured for herself and tried not to shiver at its coldness. At least she felt a little more awake.

Her mother moved to the stove, pulling lids off pans. She heaped Tamarind's plate with a breaded and fried pounded pork fillet and poured a generous river of mushroom gravy over the top. A small mountain of noodly spaetzle completed the plate.

"Here, sit, eat…and tell me why you don't look happy, either."

"It's not that I'm unhappy." Tamarind accepted the plate from her mother then perched on the nearest tall kitchen chair. She set her plate on the table and picked up her fork.

"I always know when something is on my schatze's mind." Her mother waved a finger at her. The German endearment of "sweetheart" usually warmed Tamarind, but now she felt like a kid tucked into a corner of the kitchen with a plate of food.

Tamarind managed to pop a bite of the succulent schnitzel into her mouth and savor it. "Mouth's full," she mumbled. Of course she couldn't tell Mom, or worse, Dad, about her uphill battle with the restaurant. They'd shelled out a chunk of retirement as a down payment to help her buy The Pit.

"Ha, using good manners as an excuse not to tell me. I'll know, Moms always do." Her mother glanced toward the den. "Cleo! Are you still online looking at plants?"

"Yes indeed, my love, I'm looking at beneficial nematodes as well." His voice boomed from the den. "Is that our baby girl I hear you talking to?"

"No, it's a waif, come in from the cold."

Nights like tonight, Tamarind enjoyed the fact that she still lived with her parents as the last holdout in a quartet of children to leave the roost. But tonight also, the fact made her realize how little she had to call her own. What she did have could likely slip from her fingers within six months. Instead of saying either of these things, she laughed and ate another bite of her schnitzel.

"Do you want some potato salad? Or is your plate not hot enough?" Her mother drifted back toward the stove.

"No, no. This is fine."

"Baby girl, you should see the garden I'm planning for spring." Her dad ambled into the sprawling kitchen, his six feet, five inches and broad shoulders filling the room.

"Planning already, huh?" Tamarind asked.

"Ah, that man," her mother said as she picked up the empty frying pan and sank it into a sink full of sudsy water. "That man is planning in February...February!"

"But, dear, to get Yard of the Month takes much planning, even now."

Mom started mumbling in German, shaking her head as she did so. Dad answered her in return. Tamarind chuckled at them. Two contrasts, her fair-skinned mother with her wavy blond hair and silver highlights, and her father, with skin the color of strong coffee, his dark wiry hair trimmed close to his head. They'd made it work for nearly forty years, with God's help and good humor. Thankfully, they lived in an area that didn't frown on the blending of two races in one marriage. If and when Tamarind moved out, she'd miss their banter.

"What's so funny?" her father asked as he turned to face her.

"You two."

"I'm glad we amuse you." Dad poured himself a fresh cup of coffee and joined her at the table. "Business is slow this winter, huh?"

Tamarind nodded. "Costs are up, too. Beef prices, especially."

"Sounds like you're going to need to find ways to cut costs, either that or cut personnel." Her father, a retired lieutenant colonel, knew how to run and command. Hundreds had depended on him when he was in the Army. As much as he fussed over his lawn during his retirement, she also knew that behind his jovial manner lay a good head of knowledge.

She allowed herself to sigh. "I know. When we're busy, we need all the help we can get. I just wish I could…" She almost mentioned buying the computer program, but she also knew her dad would whip out his checkbook and do it for her. She'd figure out a way to do it herself.

Dad's ringing phone intervened, and as he glanced at it, his face brightened. "It's C.J. and Marie. Hang on."

He put her brother and sister-in-law on speakerphone, and they started chiming in about the news from Missouri, the fresh pile of snow and their kids' latest antics.

"Tell them I need more pictures of the kids," said Mom, leaning close to Dad's shoulder.

"We're sending some by e-mail, Mom," boomed C.J.'s voice across the line.

Tamarind picked at the rest of her plate then slunk in the direction of the sink. She had books to read over for the restaurant.

"Tell everyone hi for me," she called out as she left the kitchen.

"Hey, Tam!" her brother said.

Her parents turned their attention back to the phone, and Tamarind headed toward her room.

She picked up the folder she'd brought home as she passed the hallway table. Somehow, she'd figure out this slow but steady leak in the restaurant's figures.

At last, after a shower and in her warm flannels, Tamarind picked up the file again but glanced at the Bible on her chest of drawers. Proverbs, the book of wisdom, lay within the covers. She'd heard of some businessmen using the Bible as a handbook, especially Proverbs. She opened to where she'd last left off reading.

*The crucible for silver and the furnace for gold,
but people are tested by their praise. Though you
grind a fool in a mortar, grinding them like grain
with a pestle, you will not remove their folly from
them. Be sure you know the condition of your
flocks, give careful attention to your herds; for
riches do not endure forever, and a crown is not
secure for all generations.*

The verse about not being able to grind folly out of a fool made her laugh. The verse about paying attention to herds and flocks made her pause. She didn't have herds or flocks, but she did have a walk-in freezer with inventory and employees who counted on her. And now, Rick showed up. He knew more than she did about the industry, but it was clear he wasn't here to help her.

What was she going to do about him? Would he aid his competition? He was a fierce competitor on the barbecue circuit, yet she knew he wouldn't hurt someone deliberately to let them lose.

She recalled what had happened in Oklahoma, not at the last competition but at one earlier last summer. She'd been hurrying to make it to the turn-in table and had tripped on someone's tent pole. She'd landed on her stomach, like a football player, holding her covered platter of chicken thighs straight out in front of her. Rick had been hurrying, too, but instead of leaving her literally in the dust, he'd stopped to help her up. They both made it to the judging tent with thirty seconds to spare.

Maybe she'd swallow her pride and ask Rick for a few pointers. He was busy, but it certainly wouldn't hurt.

She curled up on her side and read a little more of Proverbs, praying for some inspiration as she did so. Her reading turned into a dream of her and Rick running, with fools dressed as court jesters trying to trip them up.

## Chapter 4

Rick entered Starlight Community Church. Thankfully, he didn't feel out of place without a tie. What made him feel out of place were memories of attending Mass as a child, sitting on a wooden bench, trying not to kick the kneeler in front of his toes. Father Santorini scared him, too, with a shiny cue-ball head, round eyes, and ample girth. He looked like a James Bond thug masquerading in a black shirt and white collar.

His mom always told him, once he'd partaken of his First Communion, he could always go to confession. He used to make up sins so he could go to confession, just to please her, which he then felt guilty about. By the time confirmation came around in high school, he'd given up on the whole thing, much to her bitter disappointment.

He'd heard of Protestant services, had even flipped through the channels late at night to see the hucksters pitching for money in their thousand-dollar suits. It was just as much a scam as the Holy Church selling indulgences in the Middle Ages.

A belief system like that was not for him, thank you very much.

"Welcome to Starlight Community," said a familiar-sounding voice. Herb Bush stood just inside the doorway. "Your first time with us, right?"

"Hi, Mr. Bush. Yes, it is." Now he wanted to run back to his car and speed to his apartment so he could catch up on some of the sleep he'd been missing. Too late.

"Good to see ya here. Just call me Herb, though." The older gentleman clasped Rick's hand in a firm shake. "I hope you enjoy the service."

*Enjoy, huh.* This was for business, so he supposed he would enjoy it. Starlight was his new adopted town of residence, if only for a while.

Two screens that looked like miniature JumboTrons displayed a welcome message to the left and right of a simple podium.

Men's prayer breakfast at The Pit, Saturday 7 a.m.
Shut-in visits, Tuesday 9 a.m.
Choir practice, Sunday 4 p.m.
Winter cleanup, Saturday 10 a.m.

The list of activities made him blink. And he thought that all the sacraments were a lot to keep up with. However, he was just visiting here. Just visiting.

Herb joined his wife up toward the front, but Rick preferred to sit in the second row from the back. He figured he could do this once a week. It certainly seemed a lot livelier than Mass. People talked and chatted in the sanctuary, some embracing, some shaking hands.

Friendly was a good sign.

The music began as the room started to fill up with people. A familiar figure, stately and elegant, brushed past Rick's aisle. The end of a wool scarf trailed off her shoulder and caught on the edge of the wooden pew. The tug made her stop and turn.

Tamarind. Rick could only smile at her and give a half wave as she unsnagged her scarf, her green eyes wide, staring at him. "Rick…"

He shrugged. "Thought I'd check it out."

"Um, yes." She nodded, fumbling with the scarf's fringe. She shifted a Bible under her arm. Then she glanced to the front.

"Plenty of room in the back." Rick patted the empty space beside him. Tamarind slipped into the pew space and sat down next to him. Chilly air from outside clung to her coat.

She tried to slip her arms from her coat, and Rick reached for her collar. The gesture surprised even him. A faint rosy glow crept into Tamarind's cheeks.

"Thanks. I was in a hurry this morning. I overslept a little." The magenta sweater she wore accented her skin.

Rick tried not to stare. He'd never seen Tamarind dressed like this before. A knot tightened in his throat. "You're closed on Sunday."

"Yes, every Sunday." The opening music swelled, drowning out her voice. She leaned closer. "Everybody needs one day of rest."

"That can lose you a pile of cash right there." Someone on the stage was drumming a mean beat, and the congregation started clapping. Rick didn't know if he should be scared or exhilarated. Of course, the idea that Tamarind was sitting right next to him probably had a lot to do with that.

"I don't mind," was all she said. "A day of rest is good, for me and the workers."

He dropped the subject, knowing full well that talking during church was probably frowned on, even in a Protestant sanctuary. The music was…interesting. Yes, that was the best word. He'd never heard anything like it. The tempo slowed down, the congregation singing about loving God and knowing Him.

Rick glanced at Tamarind. Her eyes were closed as she sang the words, like she meant them. They'd never talked about religion on the competition trail. He'd seen her pray before lighting the grill. He likened the gesture to what some of the other barbecuers did—wearing a special necklace or clutching a special stuffed animal. Almost like a good-luck charm. Nah, he didn't need any good-luck charm to help him get the job done. He'd only come in second to Tamarind's barbecue team this summer because she'd out-cooked him.

They sat down. Good thing he'd paid attention, or he'd be standing there with his wandering mind. He opened the folded program that Herb had handed to him when he arrived—an order of service with a list of announcements that repeated the display on the screens before the music started.

Eventually came sermon time, which was different than most of the homilies Rick had ever heard. For one thing, it was a little longer. Another thing, people looked along in their Bibles. Tamarind was pretty fast in looking up the references. He didn't bother picking up a Bible from the rack in front of his knees. By the time he got to the right page, the preacher would probably be off to the next one. So he sat there, trying to look interested. He wondered if this was the best use of his time, sitting through a church service like this. His stomach growled and complained, too. In his hurry to get to the church on time, he'd skipped breakfast.

The gurgling made Tamarind smile and give a little *humph*. She glanced his way. "No breakfast?"

He shook his head and whispered, "You weren't the only one running late this morning."

"Ah." She nodded and wrote something on the back of her program. At first he thought she was going to pass him a note, like a kid in grade school. He squinted to see her handwriting:

*We love Him because He first loved us: I can't do anything to make God love me more than He does right now.*

Before she caught him looking again, Rick snapped his attention back to the preacher. Tamarind Brown, truly a woman of mystery to him. Not a religious nut. At least she didn't act like one, not that he'd seen last summer. But this...this whole church thing was something new to him.

Tamarind's mother pulled the lid off a bubbling pot on the stove. Sausage and sauerkraut. Tamarind inhaled the pungent aroma. "You like sauerkraut, Rick?" her mother asked.

"Um, I've had it before, but it's been a long time."

Rick almost squirmed where he sat at the Browns' kitchen banquette, and Tamarind stifled her laughter.

This whole situation was her fault. She had to blurt out after the service ended, "So what are you doing for lunch?"

Next thing she knew, Rick Mantovani was following her home to meet her parents. For lunch, yes, but she hadn't missed her parents' quizzical looks as she explained Rick was coming to eat with them. Tamarind always had an open invitation to invite anyone home for lunch on Sundays. That is, if she wasn't meeting up with friends herself and going out to eat.

"Mom's sauerkraut is the best, really," Tamarind said.

"Oh, the tablecloth, schatze," Mom said. "It's in the dryer. Can you go get it for the dining table?"

"We're not eating in here today?"

"No, we have company." The way her mother said *company* made Tamarind want to groan. Poor Rick.

He flung a desperate glance at her as she crossed the kitchen. "Help me," he mouthed. Tamarind responded by sticking her tongue out at him.

As she entered the utility room, she wondered where her dad had disappeared to. So far, he hadn't dragged Rick to the den to see his garden plans or grill Rick about the restaurant. That would come soon enough. *Oh Lord, please don't let him ask Rick what his "intentions" are.*

Tamarind wasn't so sure herself. As much as she liked Rick, she wasn't sure what he believed about spiritual things. Her spiritual life was important to her, probably more than anything else. She loved God, knew that

He loved her, and she wanted to please Him with her life. Not everyone believed that way.

Last summer Rick had only been a friend. He'd mentioned something about his parents being devout Catholics, but as far as his own beliefs, he'd said nothing. They hadn't gotten past their enjoyment of mutual interests and a teasing banter. Of course, she had no reason to believe that Rick thought of her as anything *but* a friend.

She'd made that mistake before. Billy Tucker had once held her heart, although he realized it too late, by the time he'd fallen for someone else. She'd been there, waiting patiently, hoping, praying that he'd wake up and see her. Of course, she didn't know what he'd been through, nearly losing his life in Iraq. Their friendship hadn't been enough, and she was left holding the meager offering of her heart, splintered in pieces because of her own hopes. Billy had never promised her anything more than friendship, and she'd nearly poisoned what they had because of her persistence.

She paused her thoughts long enough to take the tablecloth from the dryer. No, she hadn't been obnoxious in waiting for Billy. She knew better than that. This time, whatever man God brought her way, she wouldn't sink her hopes into him too soon or misread friendship for anything more. What was it she'd read in Proverbs the other night, about one of the great mysteries, of the way of a man with a maid? What attracted a man and woman together, more than mere friendship? A popular movie from her older siblings' day maintained that a man and a woman couldn't stay friends before one of them ended up wanting more than friendship. Maybe there was some truth to that. Like with Billy.

*Oh dear.* While she'd stood there in the utility room, musing about the mystery of relationships, who knows what her mother had been telling—or asking—Rick. Tamarind scurried back into the kitchen.

"The Edelweiss Club is getting ready for Valentine's Day," her mother was saying.

*Whew.* Now that was a safe subject—her mother's involvement in a local club of German ladies who'd married Americans serving overseas and followed their husbands to the States. They kept up with news from Germany and maintained traditions from their home country.

"Oh, really?" Rick glanced at Tamarind, and his warm expression made her cheeks burn.

"It's a big thing this time of year," Tamarind said, clutching the tablecloth to her chest like a feeble shield. "The Starlight and Sweethearts Night is coming up on Valentine's Day. The Edelweiss Club sponsors it as their big fund-raiser for the Wounded Warrior Project."

"I've heard of that program." Rick nodded.

"All our proceeds go to the cause," said her mother. "We have a sausage supper and a silent auction that night, and we sell Secret Sweetheart gifts that get delivered during the two weeks just before Valentine's Day. People don't know who gives the gifts until they go to the Starlight and Sweethearts night. Last year we raised almost ten thousand dollars." Her mother took down some plates from the china cabinet. "Schatze, set the table."

Tamarind smiled, shifted the tablecloth over one arm, and accepted the plates from her mother.

"What does *schatze* mean?" Rick asked.

"It's German," Tamarind replied.

"It means 'sweetheart,' " said Mom. "Tamarind has always been our little schatze, born after my Cleo and I thought we were too old to have any more children."

Tamarind asked, "Rick, could you give me a hand with the tablecloth?"

"You got it." He joined her at the entryway to the dining room. "I had no idea I'd end up getting recruited for banquet setup."

"Ha, ha." Tamarind handed him the plates. "Here. Put these on the sideboard."

"Your parents are something else." Rick reached for the edge of the tablecloth opposite the one that Tamarind held.

"That, they are." She had no idea what he thought of her, still living at home with her parents. Yes, she could have moved out, but it didn't make sense to get her own place yet, as much time as she spent at the restaurant.

"Your dad said something about going shooting after lunch?"

"Yes, he did. We both belong to the pistol club in town, but since I've had the restaurant I haven't participated much."

Oh dear. She'd hoped she'd heard Dad wrong when they first arrived at the house. Shooting? Yes, she had her concealed carry permit and often had a pistol with her when she traveled and when she worked late at the restaurant. Well, if Rick wanted to know all of Tamarind Brown, now was as good a time as any. Besides, it wasn't like he was interested.

## Chapter 5

"You ever fired a gun?" asked Cleo Brown.

Rick shook his head. "Unless you count a squirt gun, uh, no."

"We'll get you up to speed here, once we know you're not going to do anything stupid like blow off someone's foot," Cleo said.

Rick had just intended to go to the Browns' for lunch, but now here he was, with Cleo and Tamarind at The Shooting Zone just outside the Starlight city limits. A local guy had opened a range for gun enthusiasts to practice their skills. Rick tried to ponder the concept in northern New Jersey but couldn't. He was sure there must be firing ranges in his part of the country, but he'd never ventured to search for one.

Tamarind looked at him, her green eyes covered with yellow-tinted glasses. "You look nervous."

"I'm fine." He tried not to wipe his palms on his

jeans. Give him knives that could lop off a finger without effort. He knew how to handle those. But a gun? He stared at the pistol on the counter in front of him.

"We'll rent a gun for you so we can all shoot at the same time," Cleo had explained when they paid for their range time. Rick translated that as: *So you won't slow us down.* Cleo brought along what looked like a plastic toolbox, only much heavier as it was filled with ammunition.

Tamarind stood by as her father showed Rick how to load the bullets in a clip, then pop the clip into the gun.

"Do it like this, see? You smack it good with your palm, and it's loaded." Cleo wiggled the clip stuck into the handle.

Rick nodded. "I see."

"Never put your finger to the trigger if you're not ready to shoot," said Cleo. His dark, beefy hands turned the pistol and set it in Rick's right hand. "Go ahead, hang on to it. It's not going to bite you. I need to load my magazine. Tam, you going to help your young man here?"

*Tamarind must be loving this.* Rick glanced at her, but she was already working on getting her bullets loaded in a magazine. He caught her eye, and she grinned that flashy smile of hers; her cheeks flushed at her father's words. No wonder he'd accepted her invite to lunch. The more he was in Starlight, the more he wanted to spend time with Tamarind. Except he'd had to remind himself he was only here temporarily. Business came first. She knew that very well, and it showed in her own work ethic. But something in her eyes told him she'd welcome the chance to spend time with him, too.

"You ready?" Her voice held a lilt.

"I think so."

She joined him at his firing lane. "Okay, you need to chamber your first round. Then it'll be ready to fire. Watch here."

She stood close, very close, and he caught a faint whiff of the last of her perfume. This time she didn't look him in the eye as she usually did but kept her focus on the pistol he held. She took it from him, and he noticed the bandage on her finger. Good. She'd taken care of the cut from the other day.

"Pull this back until it clicks, and you're ready to fire."

"Will it kick back much when I shoot?" He found his voice again.

"It shouldn't. Not much, anyway. Just hold on as you gently squeeze the trigger." She handed the pistol back to him, her hands lending some warmth to the gunmetal.

*C'mon, Rick. Quit fooling yourself. You're trying to pretend Tamarind is just a friend, that you're only interested in Starlight for business reasons.* No wonder his business partner, Kevin, had been against the idea from the beginning and demanded that Rick use his own collateral to fund this venture.

"So, hold it like this...."

"You got it under control over there?" Cleo's voice boomed from his lane.

"Yes, Dad. Rick hasn't shot anyone yet, so we're good." At last she met his eyes. As she did so, she swallowed hard.

"Ha. Very funny." He still clutched the gun in one

hand, taking care not to point it anywhere except toward the targets at the end of the lane. He knew that much, at least.

"Okay, I'll walk you through this one." Tamarind touched his left elbow. "Face the target, don't lock your knees. Just relax."

He stood, his feet about shoulder-width apart. Knees not locked. He could handle this. "All right."

"Hold the pistol in your right hand, raise it up, pointed down the lane."

He could do this. It wasn't a knife, but he was in control as though it were.

"Now cover your right hand with your left, put your right index finger on the trigger, and fire when ready."

Rick nodded. Tamarind did this for *fun*? He squeezed, heard a pop, felt the force of the gun slamming the bullet down the alley to the paper target. His hand jerked only a little. A puff of sulfur dispersed in the air.

"Not bad. Just don't hold your breath next time." Tamarind gave his arm a playful nudge. "Now do it again and again until your magazine is empty. There should be nine more rounds."

She pranced around the low barrier to her lane and picked up her pistol. Then in flowing succession, she popped off ten rounds. Her eyes narrowed, focus honed in on the target at the end of the lane. Smoke rose from the end of her dark pistol, and she set it down. Then she pushed a button and her target came in their direction, zooming along some sort of a line.

A grin crossed her face as she smoothed back a few unruly hairs that crept from underneath her Texas Rangers ball cap. Rick's mouth went dry. What a mystery woman—sassy chef, loyal daughter, his funny friend. He kept reminding himself of the word *friend*. Then there was that thing about religion.... She didn't fit any religious mold he'd ever seen before.

"Here we go. All except one in the center." Tamarind pulled the paper off the line and replaced it with a fresh, undamaged target.

"You're good."

Tamarind shrugged and ducked her head, just a little. "Dad taught me how to shoot when I was ten. I never liked hunting—I only went once. Couldn't do it, looking at the sweet deer with big eyes. But I like target practice." She glanced at him. "You can go ahead and shoot.... Don't wait for me."

A stream of pops from a pistol behind him almost made Rick jump. Cleo had just emptied his magazine. "Don't be shy, Rick."

So with both Tamarind and her father staring at him, Rick turned back to face his own target, took aim, and reminded himself to breathe. Of course he wanted all ten shots in the center of the target. He squeezed the trigger, felt the gun jerk. Took aim again and repeated the process until he was out of bullets. The air around them smelled like Fourth of July fireworks.

His cell phone buzzed in his pocket. Rick set the gun down.

"You did good, Rick." Tamarind's wide smile made him grin like an idiot. He pulled out his phone. Kevin: So are you done playing cowboy in Texas? When are u heading back here? Don't forget the meeting on Wednesday.

Ah, reality.

* * *

Tamarind hadn't pouted since she was a young child, but now she felt as if she'd been called on the carpet for something that wasn't her fault...not entirely, anyway. She tried not to glare at the register, which for some reason decided it wasn't going to print out receipts today.

"I'm twenty-eight, not sixteen." Tamarind crossed her arms over her chest. "Don't you think I've thought of this already?"

"Schatze, your dad said this Rick was practically eating you up with his eyes. *Eating!*" Her mother's normally pale cheeks were flushed. "He's a wolf, come down to pull you out of the fold. I know his kind. Don't think I don't."

If she heard the endearment *schatze* one more time, she'd scream. Well, probably not. Her mother meant well.... Tamarind considered her next words carefully.

"Mom, nothing happened, and Dad was there. Rick is just a friend from the competitive barbecue circuit. We really hit it off last summer because we kept running into each other at the contests. He's starting a new business here in town, and he doesn't have any friends yet, really. I'm the only one he has." She ignored the wolf remark but definitely remembered the pop and sizzle of attraction she'd felt when she coached him on shooting. Maybe it was the fact of being in someone's personal space. Or maybe not. She'd felt the attraction between them before, last summer, and dismissed it quickly.

"Time for him to make plenty of friends, then." Her mother shook her head. "I just know how much you were hurt with Billy. I don't want you hurt again. Rick isn't the kind of man that'll stay around."

"I know he's not planning to stay. But he's not Billy. I haven't known him nearly as long." Tamarind looked up when the door opened. She shouldn't expect Rick to walk in the door, especially since she knew he'd flown back to New Jersey Monday morning and had an important meeting today, Wednesday. Still, her heart sank just a little.

It was John Caraway, in for lunch. The grizzled veteran was one of her favorite patrons and sat in his usual booth where a variety of friends would rotate through for coffee and free advice. He smiled and nodded at Tamarind and her mom as he headed for his space. His calming presence was welcome in The Pit.

"Be careful. I want you with the man God has for you. Right now, though, I highly doubt that's Rick Macaroni, or however you say his name."

"Mantovani." Tamarind gritted her teeth but smiled as she leaned across the counter and gave her mother a hug. "Don't worry. Because right now, I agree with you."

"I know you're busy, but I had to stop by and tell you. It's been bothering me since Sunday."

And her mother had taken *this* long to tell her? Now, that was something. Usually she gave her opinion immediately, asked for or not.

"Thanks for telling me, Mom." Tamarind waved as her mom left the restaurant. Actually, whatever was, or wasn't, going on with Rick should be low on her priority list. She'd gone over her books to see why the food costs had increased, besides the economy. She should ask Rick, but she didn't want him to see the not-so-pretty side of her business.

The Pit was ready to hit its lunchtime overdrive. Mike barked out orders from where he stood behind the pass-through. Tamarind wished she could give him a raise. She'd give all her employees a raise if she could. *Lord, I don't see how to work that out.* They all deserved some extra compensation. Plus, what if better opportunities presented themselves?

Tamarind almost stopped in midstride across the dining room. Rick wouldn't swipe her employees. Surely he wouldn't try something like that. Maybe Mom was right, that she ought to watch her back where Rick was concerned.

She'd confused infatuation with the beginnings of love before and wouldn't make that mistake again. No sirree, especially not when her restaurant was on the line. Tamarind stopped at the hand-washing station before hitting the line.

"Going okay, Mike?" she called over her shoulder.

He paused and smiled at her. "Going great. Better, now that you're here."

She blinked. "Okay…"

"I'm getting low on the brisket, didn't have a chance to check on the one resting in the smoker."

Tamarind almost sighed in relief. "I'll check on that." Plus, she needed to examine the smoker itself. She fired up the large contraption several times a week to make the next supply of beef brisket, pulled pork, or smoked chicken.

Suzie called from the front. "Hey, Tamarind! Someone's got a delivery. It's for you."

"Tell 'em to come around back." She wasn't expecting a delivery today, and all the vendors knew to bring supplies to the back door.

"It's not food. It's flowers."

Tamarind stood up straight from the sink. "I'll be right there."

She tried not to scamper to the front, mindful of Mike's stare. Sure enough, she could see a flower arrangement on the counter by the register. Suzie sneezed. "These are for you."

Gertrude Jenkins, president of the Edelweiss Club, gestured toward the enormous bouquet. "Happy Starlight and Sweethearts from the Edelweiss Club," she said. "To Tamarind Brown."

Yellow roses, at least two dozen, arranged with fern and baby's breath in a crystal vase. A card was attached. Tamarind found her voice. "Is it anonymous, or secret?"

"You'll have to open and find out." Gertrude shrugged, a half smile on her face.

"Wow, Tam, they're gorgeous." Suzie touched one of the blossoms. "I wish Greg would get me one of these. It's for a good cause, too, besides getting him out of the doghouse."

The card was square with a simple red heart on the front. She reached for it and paused. "I'll open this in the back."

"Aww," Suzie said. "You sure?"

Tamarind nodded. "I'm sure. Thanks, Gertrude."

"Not a problem. Remember, if it's a mystery gift, you'll find out who it is at the Starlight and Sweethearts Gala on Valentine's weekend." Gertrude nodded at Tamarind.

"Okay, I'll remember that." Tamarind lifted the

vase, heavy with the weight of water, crystal, and flowers. She inhaled the aroma of summertime and her mother's rose garden.

Suzie went back to her customers, and Tamarind fled to the privacy of her office. She set the vase on the one clear spot on her desk then turned her attention to the card in her hand:

*Be my Valentine, Tamarind.*
*Mike*

*Mike?*
Tamarind sank onto her office chair.

Mike appeared in the doorway. "Those sure are beautiful. Yellow roses are your favorite, aren't they?"

"Yes, yes they are. That was very thoughtful." *Thoughtful?*

He shifted from one foot to the other. Poor guy, probably tongue-tied, as was she. Mike. She never thought of him in *that* way. He was a good friend…but…

Now she knew how Billy felt. From this point on, she wouldn't give Mike any reason to think she'd be anything more than a friend to him, especially since she was his boss.

"You're a good friend, Mike."

"Well, ah, thanks, Tam. I try to be…. You, ah, deserve to be happy. I hope you will be."

She nodded. "Thank you, too. It's hard to find loyal friends, not to mention loyal employees." Wow, she was messing this one up but good.

"I have a favor to ask, if you don't mind," he said.

"Ask away, and I'll let you know if I can do it." Tamarind inhaled the scent of the roses.

"I was hoping you'd raise my pay by twenty-five cents an hour. I haven't had a raise in over a year, and right about now I could really use it." He looked her straight in the eye, his nerves over sending her the flowers evidently erased.

"I'll have to look into it. The budget is tight, as you probably know." Tamarind tried not to sigh. "You and Suzie, and the others… You're great workers. But I'm not saying no. I'm going to look into it and let you know." As if she didn't have enough matters to look into. Not that she grudged her employees the extra pay, but when she'd never really had a raise in her years of owning The Pit, it wasn't something she'd thought about much.

"Mike! Another pulled pork!" Suzie shrieked through the pass-through.

Tamarind cringed. It was definitely time to start those weekly morale meetings again, if only to remind one another of professionalism on the job. She enjoyed feeling that The Pit and its employees were like a second family, but that didn't mean they could all pretend they were in their home kitchens.

*Please, Lord, let this awkwardness with Mike go away.* Tamarind went to check on the brisket. She tried not to think of Rick. He hadn't said when he'd be back, exactly. She needed to take her mother's advice and protect herself. She had enough on her plate, especially with the restaurant.

## Chapter 6

A week in Texas might as well have been a month, as out of synch as Rick felt on his return to the Northeast. While in Texas, he'd checked his e-mail every day for restaurant reports, called and talked to the executive chefs, and kept in touch with Kevin. But this afternoon in his New Jersey office, he found his attention wandering back to Texas. A light snow fell outside the office window. He always found the sight comforting. Today, however, he wondered what the weather was like in Starlight.

Mantovani's and Pasta-Pasta were "his" concepts transformed into very different culinary hot spots, but this latest venture claimed his immediate focus. He already had plans to return to Texas in two weeks to see the contractor's progress and work on his local business networking contacts. This was typical—the "honeymoon" period for a restaurant. Visions of the interior lit his dreams. The Rick's Fabulous Western Barbecue would be classy barbecue, without any of the chain steak house, cookie-cutter decor.

Did Tamarind know of any good flea markets or antique stores in the area? He figured he'd find some great accessories there, although summer might be a better time to shop. If he had a bigger budget, he could hire a designer. Maybe he would. He wrote down "hire designer?" on his notepad. There was a college nearby. They might have some design students who'd be willing to take on designing his restaurant for a good price.

"So we're heading into a strong first quarter," Kevin was saying on the other side of the table.

"It looks that way so far," Seamus Quinn, their accountant, said.

"What about your project in Texas?" Kevin gave Rick a piercing look.

"The interior demo started this week, and the contractor said that barring any unforeseen structural or electrical issues, they should be able to have the framing up by the time I fly down again at the end of next week."

"You sound pleased with yourself," Kevin said.

"I am. I don't care if you think this is a bad idea. I'm going to make it work."

"Connecticut, I could see you opening a place there. Or maybe upstate, if you wanted to have a more rustic setting for a restaurant." Kevin shook his head. "But Texas?"

They'd been through this before. "My building costs are lower in Texas than here, and you know it." Rick cast a glance at his accountant. "Seamus, I'm on budget at the moment."

"Well, uh, yes…"

"You've only just started. You admit that yourself." Kevin sighed. "Look, I'm not trying to be negative here."

"Could've fooled me."

"But seriously, man. There are a million things that could go wrong. And you can definitely *not* afford to be down there full-time, especially when we've got two other restaurants here." Kevin's forehead wrinkled with concern.

"I know." Rick nodded. "You're right. I value your opinion, especially since I get sucked into the artistic and culinary sides of things, and the checkbook sort of can take a backseat."

"Don't be too hard on yourself. We're in this for the long haul, and so far, so good. In fact, I wanted to let you know—I've already started scouting possible ventures for a Lower East Side location. If we find the right place, we could be up and running in eighteen months." Now Kevin looked triumphant.

Rick took a deep breath and released it. "Another location, in eighteen months?"

"You said you wanted to do a nouveau Italian someday. This would be an intimate eighteen-seat restaurant, reservations only, a rotating menu…something exclusive."

"How exclusive?"

"So exclusive we'll have the latest James Beard winners lining up to work as sous chefs."

Rick snorted at Kevin's remark. "That's stretching it a bit. I'm not sure that's the angle I'd like to go for." He and Kevin had had their share of go-rounds over the years they'd worked together, so he was used to this interplay. However, a thread of tension wound a little tighter in the air tonight.

Seamus closed his folder and stood. "I assume you're done with my reports?"

"Yes, thanks," Rick said. "We'll be in touch, of course."

"I'll see you gentlemen soon." Seamus nodded and left the room.

"So, back to the elephant in the room." Kevin took a sip from his coffee cup. "Something's up with you since last summer. I figured you were just learning a new cooking style, working those barbecue competitions to bring back and put your own Manhattan twist on things."

"I was. I did." Rick reached around in his brain for the right words. "I decided I wasn't going to try to 'do' barbecue up here. Some people look at it as a novelty, not as high-end cuisine. They think it's something you do in backyards in the summer. In other parts of the country, it's an art form. I think maybe the ones in Texas might appreciate a Manhattan spin on their dishes."

"That makes no more sense than your original idea."

"Why are you fighting me on this?"

"I'm not…. You've just always been more reasonable and made good business decisions before. This feels like too much of a risk, financially and time wise." Kevin frowned again. "I think you should put your energies into the nouveau Italian place instead."

"I'll prove you wrong. I'm not using any of our funds on this, just so you know."

"Of course you're not. If you did, then I'd insist you pay our partnership back."

"And I would. So in the meantime, if you're scouting out that 'nouveau Italian' spot, don't do it on our dime. I don't know if I want to go in that direction anymore."

"All right then, I won't."

"Good."

They both retreated to their respective offices. Yes, they'd butted heads before but never over so many things at once. Kevin was a good voice of reason, and they'd worked together ever since opening Mantovani's ten years ago. But sometimes, it was good to ignore the voice of reason and go with your gut.

As Rick began the commute home, his thoughts drifted back to Tamarind and Starlight. The new project clamored for some brain time, too. Everything about the place—the location, the fact that he could see Tamarind regularly, the idea that he might actually get to wear flip-flops before Easter—all appealed to him.

His phone buzzed. *Mom.* "Hey, Ma."

"You're coming for supper, right?" Her voice sounded tinny on the cell phone.

It wasn't Sunday, but... "Yes, I can come by."

"You forgot, didn't you?" Her tone chided him.

"Dad's retirement!" He slapped his forehead, and the sharp thud made others on the subway look at him. "I'll be there. Yes. Do you need me to bring anything?" He always asked, and even if she said no, he'd always pick up a loaf of bread from the bakery down the street from where they lived.

"Nah, just bring yourself. And hurry up about it." Tart words, but her voice sounded warm.

"That's what I meant."

"I…I'll think about it." Tamarind gave the group her best smile. "I'll see about your coffee right away." She didn't look for her mother's reaction as she stepped back toward the drink station. What she wouldn't think about was the signature on the card for the flowers. Mike. Still hard to wrap her head around that one.

"I'm sorry." Suzie glided into the drink station. "I know it's a mess. I'll clean it up as soon as I can. But those ladies have me running."

"Yes, I know you will." Tamarind touched her arm. "Relax. My mom's group is clamoring for more coffee, by the way."

"I know." Suzie paused for a moment and huffed a sigh. "Sweet ladies, but they wear me out."

"I completely sympathize with you." Tamarind laughed and headed for the kitchen. The toe of her shoe caught on a nick in the linoleum, but she didn't stumble or come close to falling. The linoleum, like dozens of other things about The Pit, nagged at her.

She checked out the line. "You doing okay, Mike?"

"Got it good, Tam." The grill sizzled, the fryer bubbled. "You need a break, feel free, boss. I've got things under control here."

The previous dinnertime frenzy was winding down as night fell and the temperature dropped. Tamarind was waiting for Starlight to have its first ice storm of the winter that would shut the town down for a day or two. It happened some years, and other years, no.

She entered the office and sank onto her chair. She might as well check the voice message from Rick on her phone.

"*Hey, Tamarind.*" His voice sounded muffled, strained, tired. She'd never heard a tone like that from him before. Usually Rick was full of energy, enthusiasm. *"I know you pray. So, when you do, could you pray for my dad? He's had a heart attack, and it doesn't look good. Thanks. Uh... You take care. Talk to you soon."*

It was nearly eight thirty, which made it nine thirty on the East Coast. She'd call him tomorrow. Rick had asked her to pray. She'd do that, for sure. Right now, though, she wished she were in New Jersey with her friend. She remembered the scare with her dad a couple of years ago. *Hang on, Rick.* She almost dialed him back but decided against it.

# *Chapter* 7

$O$n his first morning back in Starlight, Rick awoke to a gray, icy world outside. Good thing he'd flown back yesterday, although reluctantly. He'd delayed his return for three days, long enough to make sure his father went home from the hospital and his parents had everything they needed. Donny and Graciela assured him they'd check on Mom and Dad.

"Go," his father had told him. "You're a businessman, and I'll be fine. I have plenty of people watching over me." But his father had spoken the words while lying downstairs in a hospital bed, unable to climb the steps to the second floor of their home.

Rick tiptoed down the hallway, trying not to shiver. Somehow, the thermostat had quit working overnight. He flipped a light switch. No power. Great. He had enough to do today without waiting around for a repairman to arrive. Worse, he'd forgotten to set the coffeepot when he arrived from the airport. Not that it would have mattered if the power was out. At least he had a gas stove. He picked up the teakettle and turned on the water. Nothing. He tried the other faucet. Nothing. What in the world? He'd paid the water bill. Rick went into the bathroom and tried that faucet. Nothing. Then a rattling noise somewhere under the floor, and more nothing. Frozen pipes.

Which reminded him he ought to check on Millicent House. The structure had been demolished on the inside to pave the way for the restaurant kitchen and main dining room. If *those* pipes were frozen in an unheated building, that could be an even worse situation. He opened the cabinet doors to coax some unfrozen air to the pipes under the sink.

Outside his front door, ice covered the tree limbs, fence posts, and wiring. Some wires were down, which explained the power outage. Rick took a few steps and skidded, almost slipping onto his back. He made a retreat to the kitchen and snatched up the box of salt in the cabinet. Then he sprinkled the salt on his steps. That's all he needed—for him or someone else to break an ankle.

He managed to open his car after sliding to the driver's door and chipping away at the ice. Once he got the engine started, he sat there for fifteen minutes waiting for the defroster to kick in. An icy dampness hung in the air outside, but Rick didn't shiver. He was used to freezing weather. He'd slogged through well over two dozen New Jersey and Manhattan winters. You sort of dug out, hunkered down, and moved along with life as best you could.

At last he crept along the street in his rental car. A few vehicles had passed the same way before him, leaving icy furrows covering the asphalt underneath. Slow and steady, and he'd get to Millicent House in one piece.

All he needed was to negotiate one turn onto Main Street, and he'd be almost there.

Movement caught his periphery vision. Someone's dog, its head darting anxiously side to side, trotted directly in front of him. The dog's breath made little puffs in the air. Rick tapped the brakes. The mutt darted back the way he came.

The car slid. Rick turned the wheel.

Too late… The car moved with a mind of its own, curving into Main Street. Rick gripped the wheel, attempting to steer.

No response.

The slide took him toward the corner and close to a drainage ditch. If he fell in, he'd never get out.

Rick pumped the brakes as the vehicle headed toward the stop sign. He hit the brakes again. The car's rear end slid over the curb. The front end followed.

He crunched to a halt. Rick found himself at an angle, the front end of the car nosing into the narrow spillway.

Unbelievable. Rick smacked the steering wheel with his palm. He turned off the ignition and set the emergency brake. He tried not to laugh at the futile gesture— there was nowhere else for the car to slide.

He exited the car, debating about walking back to his cold and dark apartment. He pulled out his phone. He hadn't called Tamarind yet since he'd been back in Starlight. They'd talked the morning after Dad was admitted to the hospital. Her words had been comforting, reassuring. He realized how much he'd missed her, and he really wanted to be back in Texas. But the pull to be close to his family made the distance between Texas and New Jersey seem a lot farther now.

Rick punched Tamarind's number on speed dial. She answered at the first ring.

"Rick?" Laughter in the background. "Where are you?"

"I'm back…and stranded, sort of." His breath made puffy clouds in the icy air. He tried not to let his teeth chatter.

"Where are you?"

"At the corner of Cedar and Main."

"What in the world are you out driving for? The roads are sheets of ice."

He loved her cranky tone of voice and couldn't help the chuckle that escaped. "The power's out at my place, plus my pipes are frozen. So I thought I'd go check on the restaurant. And my rental car slid into the ditch." He glanced around for the mutt, who paused at the opposite corner before skittering down the sidewalk and away.

"Unbelievable. Stay right there. Uncle Herb's going to come get you."

"I'm not going anywhere, believe me." He wasn't sure how Uncle Herb could help him, though. "Where are you? At The Pit?"

"No way. The whole town is pretty much shut down until it thaws. Although I wish I could've opened. The power grid is out, too." Tamarind sighed. "I'm at Justine and Billy Tucker's place. They're up on the hill and have a generator. Uncle Herb will bring you here."

"Okay. But I don't want him to go to any trouble and possibly have an accident himself. I can walk back to my place." He had a feeling his words were feeble against her insistence.

"Too late. He's already on his way. He drives a tow truck, and it's pretty heavy duty. So is Uncle Herb." Her laugh warmed him. "Well, I guess I'll see you soon."

"Yes, soon." He almost added, "I've missed you," but those three simple words wouldn't come out.

Rick waited for nearly twenty icy minutes. A few spits of sleet fell from the gray sky above. He scanned the roadway. A solitary vehicle crept along Main Street. A massive tow truck, its engine growling, glided to a stop.

The driver's window lowered. "You picked a fine morning to go for a drive, young man."

"Mr. Bush…"

"It's Herb, remember." The older man opened the truck door and stepped cautiously onto the street. "Looks like you've got a situation here."

"Yes, I do, Herb." His face flamed, but he straightened his shoulders. "I'm used to driving in snow."

"But not ice. This is a whole different combination of $H_2O$. We'll leave your car here. It'll keep until it thaws."

"You sure it won't get ticketed or towed?"

"I know Chief Keller. I'll tell him you didn't abandon your vehicle. Hopefully they won't ticket it. They shouldn't. More important things to tend to in town right now, anyway." Herb waved him toward the truck. "C'mon. There's a mammoth pot of chili waiting for us on the stove."

Soon they were heading toward a part of Starlight

that Rick hadn't visited yet. A gentle sloping street took them up along a ridge, with only a little protest from the tow truck and gritting of teeth by Herb as he shifted gears. The stately homes spoke of elegance, with views of the town below.

"Our Tamarind's glad you're back. Lit up like a Christmas tree when you called." Herb's tone made Rick glance at the older man. "She's a sweet girl. People can't help but love her. But she's special. She deserves someone special, too."

How in the world could he respond to that? "I think so, too, Herb. She's definitely special. People are drawn to her, and I don't blame them." The heater in the tow truck was working overtime. Rick tugged at his sweatshirt collar.

"You know, we have a men's Bible study at The Pit every Thursday at 6 a.m., if you'd like to join us."

"Ah, thanks." Church on Sunday—now that he could do. But trying to read a Bible at six o'clock in the morning? It might as well be written in Greek, for all he could understand it. He couldn't remember reading a Bible, ever. The church's missal from his altar-boy days probably didn't count, although he seemed to recall some verses listed in it.

"We're not sponsored by any particular denomination. We even let Baptists in. Or so my Lutheran brother in the Lord likes to joke." Herb chuckled.

"What about a nonreligious former Catholic?" The words slipped out as if on ice.

"Them, too, son." Herb glanced his way. "So, you don't go to church much, then?"

"Not really. I usually sleep. Or work. It depends."

"Uh-huh. Well, lots of people do." They pulled up at a driveway with no fewer than four vehicles. "Just do me a favor…."

"What's that?"

"Be up front with our Tamarind. I know she likes you a lot. I love her like she was my own kin. But she wants and needs a good Christian man who shares her beliefs. You're a good man, from what I can see so far. You seem to be a hard worker. But I could picture your opposing beliefs pulling you apart."

"Herb, I've been honest with her. If it's only our beliefs that conflict, maybe we can work it out."

"Fair enough. I'm not so sure that'll work so well, but I appreciate your honesty." Herb offered his hand, which Rick shook. "Now, mind the walk as you go in. Billy put down sand, but there are probably some slick spots."

Rick nodded. All he'd expected was a ride to safety and warmth from a new friend. He hadn't expected to feel as if he'd been measured and found lacking. But the decision would be up to Tamarind. Practically speaking, he couldn't see how things could work between them, religion aside.

"Another ice storm refugee, safely delivered," Uncle Herb called out as the front door opened.

Tamarind sat up straighter on the cushioned leather couch in Justine and Billy's den, where a fire blazed in the cut-stone fireplace. *Rick!* She raised her hand and touched her hair. Like it mattered. Her heart pounded. She'd missed him. A lot. Even more so since talking to him after his father's heart attack.

"That's it, Herbert Bush!" Aunt Azalea hollered from

the kitchen. "No more goin' out in that ice. If I have to hide your keys, I will. Sorry, Tamarind."

Tamarind stood. She might as well see Rick. Laughter rang out from the dining room, where a fierce game of Mexican train dominoes was under way between Liann and Justine, plus their husbands, Jake and Billy. Tamarind had felt like an extra around the couples, so she contented herself by alternating between reading a novel by the fireside and poring over the restaurant's books. It figured. Her parents *would* pick the week of an ice storm to go on a cruise. She found herself envying them.

She tried not to rush to the entryway to meet Rick but found herself speeding there anyhow. "Welcome back." She hugged him, feeling the cold that clung to his jacket. He surprised her with a soft kiss on her right temple.

"I missed you," he whispered.

Tamarind nodded, wanting to prolong the hug but thought better of it. Something had changed between the last time they'd seen each other and now.

"Aunt Azalea's made some chili, and the corn bread's ready to come out of the oven." She gestured over her shoulder.

"I'm gonna go calm my wife down." Uncle Herb nodded at both of them. "I trust you'll make introductions?"

"Sure will." Tamarind allowed herself to tug on Rick's sleeve. "I'll take your coat. Come meet Justine and Billy, plus Liann and Jake." She led him toward the dining room as Uncle Herb headed for the kitchen.

As soon as they entered, Liann's eyebrows shot almost to the top of her forehead.

"Hey, y'all, this is Rick Mantovani," said Tamarind.

"The power is out at his place. This is Billy and his wife Justine, and this is their home. And this is Billy's brother, Jake, and his wife Liann."

"Nice to meet all of you." Rick nodded. "Thanks for letting me hang out with you today."

"Welcome to our home." Billy rose to shake Rick's hand. "I hear you're going to be opening a restaurant this spring." They made a contrast, Billy's tall strong physique and sandy blond buzz cut, and Rick's wiry yet muscular frame and shock of dark hair.

Trust Billy to get straight to the point. Tamarind smiled.

"I'm working on it. I didn't realize Texas had such wintry weather," Rick said.

"Sometimes we'll get an ice storm like this. We usually just stay home and wait it out. Doesn't slow us down more than a day or two." Billy motioned toward the table. "You're welcome to join the game."

"Ah, well..." Rick began.

"I'm actually going to be picking Rick's brain in the den, if y'all don't mind," Tamarind interjected. "Restaurant stuff... It's not often he and I are both *not* working."

"When *aren't* you working?" Liann asked. "Even talking restaurant business today is working."

"I know.... Maybe after we eat, I'll jump in on a game." She glanced at Rick, who looked like he would rather be in the kitchen, or out sliding on the ice, or getting a root canal, than playing a game. At her words, he seemed to relax—just a little.

"Make yourself at home, go right ahead. We're almost done here, and then Aunt Zalea will serve up the chili," said Justine. A squeal came from the pack 'n' play in the corner, and B.J., Billy and Justine's nine-month-old son, made his presence known. "Hey, cutie." Justine reached for him, and he held his little arms up toward her.

Tamarind ignored the pang inside. Someday, she'd love having a family, but that wouldn't likely happen for a long time. She'd grown up in a loving home full of laughter, two parents who raised her and her siblings with love and boundaries, and wouldn't settle for less for her own future family. Right now, though, she had to get Rick's help with the restaurant, or she'd lose what she'd built so far. Love? Definitely low on her priority list at the moment.

"Here, follow me." She glanced at Rick as she led him away from the dining room and to Justine and Billy's den. Their wedding photo graced the space above the mantel. It didn't hurt anymore that Billy and Justine had ended up together. God had His hand in that situation, much as it hurt at the time for Tamarind to see it coming.

She sank onto the leather couch she'd vacated just minutes before, and Rick took up the rest of it. The atmosphere before the fire belonged in some romantic movie. Now, what to talk about? She practically forced Herb to slide him over to Justine and Billy's. For some reason, her tongue refused to cooperate at the moment.

"So," Rick began.

"So," she parroted back and smiled at him. "You can thank me for sending someone to rescue you later."

A smile quirked the corners of his lips. "I'll thank you now.... Thank you. Although I would have managed somehow."

"This is much better than a freezing apartment. Admit it. I'm glad I'm here instead of at my parents' house."

"Yes. Much, much better." The leather cushion squeaked as Rick shifted on the couch.

Tamarind's mouth went dry. She snatched up the books. "I really, really need your help with these books. That is, if you don't mind taking a look at them?"

Rick leaned closer and looked at the ledger. "Ah, your books. You said you'd had trouble with your costs."

She nodded. "My suppliers have all raised their prices in the last six months. It happens. The economy's been like a yo-yo, with the drought conditions here in Texas combined with the fluctuating fuel prices to truck supplies in."

"When was the last time you raised prices?" Rick took the ledger from her and started paging through the figures.

"About fifteen months ago. Fifty cents on entrées. Plus I only include a free side salad with beef dishes now, not every entrée. Do you think I need to raise prices again? A lot of my customers are retirees on fixed incomes. I'd hate to do that to them." Tamarind felt the urge to get up and poke the fire but made herself stop.

"Have you ever sat down and figured out your cost per dish? If it's costing you more than you make on a dish, you ought to consider dropping it from the menu if you're not going to raise the price." Rick paused at one page. "You spent over *two thousand* dollars on beef last month?"

Tamarind nodded. "It adds up, between the whole briskets and the ribs and the ground chuck."

"But do you know how many portions you sold, total, of all those beef items?"

"Uh, no. I could look it up on the tickets."

"Tamarind." Rick shook his head. "That would take more time than you can afford. I know it's killing you that your place is closed today. It's costing you money. You can't afford the time to go through those tickets and itemize dishes one by one."

"You're right. I can't." Her face flushed, and she studied the flickering flames. He probably thought she was extremely lame. Here he was, big-time chef, owner of two—soon to be three—restaurants. He'd been to a renowned culinary school.

"If you don't get a handle on this, you're going to sink." Rick looked thoughtful for a moment. "I hate to tell you this, but I think one of your employees might be stealing from you. Did you ever consider that possibility?"

"No. I highly doubt it. I've known most of them for years. Even my new prep cook, Javier, is the son of an old family friend." Ludicrous. She wasn't going to be suspicious of her employees. If there was no trust, how could she depend on them to get the work done for her?

"I think you need to think about that. Sometimes we can't ignore a logical explanation, no matter how unwelcome it is."

Theft? By one of her own? She nodded then shifted to the edge of the couch, placing her head on her hands. "I didn't... I didn't think it would be this hard."

"What's that?"

"Running a restaurant."

"How long have you been open?"

"The Pit's been open since the seventies, but my father helped me buy it four years ago when the first owner retired. I'll probably be paying on it forever." She tried not to sigh.

"So, why choose barbecue? Why a restaurant? Why not cook for your friends, or operate a catering business?"

She tried not to bristle at his words. "Why not? I learned from my parents. I didn't go to culinary school, not like you did. My...my grandfather ran a barbecue restaurant in Kansas City years ago. He died when I was five, and the family sold the place. Dad always talked about that restaurant, but he had a career in the Army. Maybe part of him regrets not going into the family business, but he did pass his cooking gene to me. I can't imagine doing anything else. Plus, Starlight needs a place like The Pit. I'm not a chain or a franchise, and I don't want it to be." Her tone rose a little, and she took a deep, calming breath.

"Easy, girl." He placed his hand on her shoulder. "I'm on your side. I've never wanted to do anything else, myself. When the dinner rush is in full gear, and I look out at the floor and see the smiles and hear the laughter... it's then that I know I'm doing what I was meant to. We were never told it would be easy."

"No, we weren't." She tried to swallow around the lump in her throat, and her eyes burned. She rarely gave tears permission to make an appearance and wasn't going to let them now.

"I understand. I do." He reached up and touched her cheek. "Tamarind, please don't cry."

She settled back on the couch cushion and shrugged. "I'll be—"

Then Rick was kissing her, holding her close in the circle of his arms. Two tears squeezed from her eyes as her mind, her heart, and everything else seemed to go topsy-turvy. Tamarind wrapped her arms around his shoulders and kissed him back. He worked out, she could tell, as his arms tightened around her.

*Restaurant? What restaurant?*

She pulled away first, trying to catch her breath, their foreheads touching. The den's temperature had to have reached one hundred degrees, at least.

"Better now?" he asked her, his voice low.

"I… Yes… No… I don't know." *This* was why she'd pulled out the ledgers, and her shoddy defense against her attraction to him had crumbled.

A shadow blocked the den's entryway. "Chili's ready!" Liann called out.

Tamarind glanced at her friend, whose eyes had rounded and filled with questions. Yes, she'd definitely need time for girl talk. Later. Tamarind tried to stand, but her legs had turned into Jell-O. Rick stood first then pulled Tamarind to her feet.

"I'm ready for chili," he said.

Tamarind nodded, not meeting his eyes. Forget the sensation of Jell-O. She'd landed not just in the deep end of the pool but was dog-paddling over the Mariana Trench without a life preserver in sight.

## Chapter 8

The heat from Tamarind's kiss had surrounded Rick until the power came back on and the pipes thawed out the following afternoon. Her sweetness covered the heart of a passionate woman. He regretted, for a few seconds, kissing her without a warning. At the moment, it was the only thing he could think of to keep her from dissolving into a pile of tears. He pulled into the driveway of Millicent House to see what the workers had accomplished since he'd been away.

He set the car in Park and paused for a moment. Who was he kidding, though? Tamarind had set herself *not* to cry. She was strong. He knew that. Nope, kissing her had been his feeble effort to defuse some of the tension between them. She'd been wound tighter than a piano string. He knew she was attracted to him. This was only a simple kiss, not a marriage proposal or a hint that he wanted anything more. Truthfully, Rick didn't

hand out kisses. He hadn't made time for romantic en-
tanglements, especially not on the job. Casual dating,
he'd learned, didn't end well. Usually one of the parties—in his case, the woman he was dating—ended up
wanting more commitment than he was ready to give.
His businesses claimed more time than any spouse.

Tamarind hadn't answered her phone since they'd left
the Tuckers' house, with Herb giving him a ride back to
his place that evening, along with a bowl of chili to tide
him over after he refused a place at the Bushes' guest
room. He did agree to at least try going to the men's
Bible study. Herb mentioned that Ray Woods, the head
of the Exchange Club in town, was a regular attender.
Going to Bible study was a logical business move, so
long as Rick's alarm clock cooperated.

*Fine.* Maybe Tamarind would return his calls, or
not. In the meantime, he had a restaurant to renovate
and open. He left the car and entered Millicent House
through the back door to find only the kitchen area
gutted to the studs. The rest of the downstairs was still
intact and sporting its 1970s charm. They'd only accomplished *this* in a week and a half? Unbelievable. Even
with the ice storm delay, they should have at least had
the entire downstairs gutted and the wiring brought up
to code, if needed.

He pulled out his phone to call the contractor, who'd
better hurry up and get himself over to the job site
today. He had a missed call from Tamarind. He almost
hit Send to return the call then decided against it. Instead, he dialed another local number and got a voice
mail greeting him.

"Hello, Mrs. Jenkins? This is Rick Mantovani. I'd

placed an order with the Edelweiss Club for two dozen roses not quite two weeks ago. Were those delivered? Please call and let me know. Thanks."

Tamarind shoved away the niggling guilt over leaving the restaurant for the afternoon and sank deeper into the chair at Chin Mae Rivers' nail salon. "I'm going to be no good the rest of the day, you know."

"You need to give yourself an afternoon off every once in a while." Liann Tucker had no problem relaxing at her perch on the pedicure chair. "I'm grateful for an early out from school today. I think the teachers are sometimes happier about it than the students."

"Now, *that* I believe." Tamarind's feet practically shrieked with joy at being soaked in the hot footbath.

"So, what's with you and Chef Rick?" Liann asked.

Yes, here was the first question, right on schedule. Although she should appreciate Liann's protectiveness, since Tamarind had run interference for Liann when her ex-fiancé followed her to Starlight.

"I don't know...."

"You were mighty, *mighty* cozy in Justine's den the other day." Liann opened her eyes and looked in Tamarind's direction.

"He kissed me, Li, and I kissed him back. And I shouldn't have." Tamarind covered her eyes. "I was sort of upset about the restaurant, and... I don't know...." The scenario had replayed itself in her mind until at least two the following morning.

"Oh dear... On one hand, I'd be happy for you. But on the other..."

"I keep telling myself, it was just a kiss. No big deal.

But I just don't go around kissing random men. We're not dating. We can't. For several reasons."

"Okay, I can think of a few obvious reasons…. But you tell me."

"For one thing, we're both super busy. He's only here in Texas to open his restaurant. Once it's up and running and he has a manager to take care of it for him, he'll be going back to New Jersey. It started out as a friendly competition between us, but now there's something else that wasn't there before. I'm afraid of messing up a good friendship and possibly a business association. Not only that…" Tamarind knew the other reason would probably hurt Rick, or at the very least offend him. "I…I don't want to be romantically involved with a man who's not a Christian…and I don't think Rick is."

"Ah, I see…." Liann nodded. "Have you talked about your faith with him, and how important it is to you?"

"No…not really. He knows I pray, and he's been at church. You saw him that one day he came, didn't you?" Tamarind wiggled her toes in the bath. If only a massage would ease away the knots in her mind. "He asked me to pray for his father after he had the heart attack, so I did. I know his mom's a very devout Catholic. Rick told me once that he sort of left that all behind in his teen years. Plus, the restaurant business isn't very conducive to regular church attendance."

"I imagine it wouldn't be. But you know that, at least for us, being a Christian isn't based on church attendance."

"I know that." Tamarind tried not to sigh. "But how do you think it would sound if I said, 'Look, Rick. You're not a Christian, so I can't date you.' It's like I'm saying I'm too good for him, that he doesn't measure up to my standards. I believe that people who have different core beliefs can end up being torn apart from each other, the closer a relationship gets. On a casual friend level, it's not that big a deal." Footsteps entered the pedicure alcove, and Tamarind looked up.

"You two comfortable?" asked Liann's aunt, Chin Mae. "I see you need to talk. You want me to come back in a few minutes?"

Liann glanced at Tamarind. "Sure, that would be fine. We're not in a hurry."

"Okay then. You relax. I make a pot of tea." Chin Mae scurried off to the main floor of the nail salon.

"That's my aunt," Liann said. "A pot of tea cures most ills. Anyway, I think you should listen to her."

"What do you mean?"

"Relax. Talk to Rick. Get the awkwardness out in the open, and deal with it. Maybe he's not that serious. Maybe it was just that…just a kiss. If you agree to be good friends from here on out, that'll be one less painful conversation you have."

"Maybe so. He *did* try calling me a few times, but I didn't know what to say, so I didn't answer." Tamarind leaned her head back on the headrest and tried not to groan.

"He called you. That's a good sign. At least he's being adult about it and wanting to talk."

Now Tamarind felt a tad foolish. She'd made Mount Everest out of a little dirt clod. "True. Except I called him back this morning, and he didn't answer."

"Ah. Well, give it time. You're both, like you said, super busy."

"That we are. Oh, Li, which reminds me. You wouldn't believe what my mother did."

"I *can* imagine, and that scares me. What did she do?"

"She volunteered me to emcee at Starlight and Sweethearts on Saturday night. As if I don't have enough to do."

"That's *wonderful*. Great exposure for your business, too."

"Ha, that sounds like something Rick would say."

"He sounds pretty business savvy."

"That he is. But sweet, too, in an unpolished way." Tamarind yawned. "I could just go right to sleep here."

"I'll wake you up if you start snoring."

At that, Tamarind couldn't resist a smile as she shifted on the cushioned chair. *Rick, please call me back. And Lord, I should spend more time praying for him. He's a friend, and I'd like for him to know You, too.*

## Chapter 9

Rick tucked his new business cards into his shirt pocket as he entered the Starlight Civic Center. Decorated in shades of red, white, and pink, the large main ballroom looked like candy canes and Pepto-Bismol were fighting for control of the space. A deejay was playing some country tunes, and the civic center floor was covered with round tables that surrounded a Texas star on the stained concrete.

A lady at the reception desk took Rick's supper ticket and greeted him. "The silent auction is on the wall to your left, and refreshments and light hors d'oeurves to the right for our meet-and-greet before supper begins," she said.

"Thank you," he replied as she slid a program across the counter toward him. Tonight, Tamarind would find out that he'd sent her the two dozen yellow roses. Did he regret the decision to send them? Maybe, just a little. It seemed like a good idea at the time, but since the ice storm, he realized he needed to chill out a little, so to speak.

He ambled over toward the beverages. Sweet iced tea, unsweetened iced tea, a lineup of sodas and sugar-free alternatives, plus coffee. Iced tea, in the middle of February? He settled for a coffee then passed through the milling guests to the silent auction items. One caught his eye—"Dinner for two, value up to $45, The Pit." Other items included nail care and massage from a local spa, free oil change, a bakery offering a year's worth of bread and rolls (limit one loaf or dozen per week, value $100), business cards or wedding invitations from a local printer.

Rick opened his program—guest speaker, Billy Tucker, former staff sergeant, United States Army. Rick's benefactor during the ice storm. He hadn't had the chance to speak to Billy after that day of chili and unending board games and dominoes. Billy worked many hours for his nonprofit and on his handcrafted cowboy boots, plus he had his little baby and his wife. Tamarind had said that Billy was severely wounded in Iraq and almost died but had come home to recover and then open a retreat for wounded soldiers and their families. He had to give the guy credit for being so resilient.

"Rick."

Tamarind's voice made him turn around. She stood there in a red dress that made her skin tone glow and almost made him run for a cup of ice water. No, make that a gallon of ice water, poured over him head to toe. She fidgeted from one high heel to the other. Her legs had to be half a mile long, at least, with the hemline skimming her knee. He tore his focus away from her legs. A simple gold chain with crystal beads glittered above her neckline.

"Hey there." He took a sip of coffee to clear his throat and burned it instead. He coughed.

"You okay?"

"I'm fine. Fine. You look...more than fine. Wow." Come to think of it, he'd never seen her dressed like this before, not even on Sunday mornings for church. Although on Sundays she always looked nice.

"I'm, um, emceeing tonight, so I figured I needed to dress up." She pushed a strand of her hair out of her eyes. "I remember why I've only worn these heels once."

"Well, you're going to do great." He wanted to say more but stopped himself and gave his singed throat a break.

"I'm glad you came. If you're looking to meet people for your business connections, this is the place to be." She glanced toward the tables. "The mayor's here, and you already know Gertrude Jenkins. Plus the Exchange Club, the Rotary Club, and representatives from the American Legion, too. We all like to get involved in causes, and this one is special to a lot of us personally." Movement by his elbow made Tamarind stand up straighter.

"Hey, y'all. I made it," said a male voice.

Billy Tucker, wearing his dress uniform, with his dazzling wife, former A-list actress and now TV show host Justine Campbell—make that Tucker now, for a couple of years. She held a wiggling, much smaller version of Billy on her hip.

"Billy, Justine." Tamarind gave Justine a hug. "Gertrude wants me to make sure you know you're all at the head table."

"Oh, great." Billy rolled his eyes but laughed. "I'm fine, just sitting at a regular table at ground level, not up on a platform."

"I know you are, but...you know Gertrude."

"Of course we do." Justine plucked Billy's sleeve. "Just humor her. We don't get to make a fuss over you often enough. And I'm the one who'll be grappling with a nine-month-old in front of the whole town."

"I know better than to argue with a determined German lady." Billy shook his head and glanced at Rick. "Rick, good to see you."

He shook Billy's hand. "Thanks again for letting me wait out the storm at your place."

"Not a problem. I hope that was the last of the bad weather for us this winter. Although one year, I remember we had four inches of snow on Easter."

"Really?" Rick shook his head.

"I kid you not." He smiled at his wife. "Well, let's not disappoint Gertrude."

They headed in the direction of a platform at one end of the hall where a podium flanked by a pair of long tables had been set up, festooned with red-and-white draped fabric. Before they reached the platform, a short Asian woman swooped toward them, pulling the baby into her arms.

"There goes Aunt Chin Mae. That's Liann Tucker's aunt." Tamarind laughed. "Never passes up a chance to cuddle and spoil a little one." Rick watched as the older woman bounced the baby on her hip and toward her own table.

"That's nice, how you all take care of each other like family even though you're not related." That was one of the things Rick liked most about Starlight.

The main lights on the ceiling dimmed, and smaller twinkle lights appeared, like stars studding the ceiling.

"Oh. That's my cue. I need to run, or not trip as I get onto the platform." Tamarind flashed Rick a smile and skimmed across the floor on her heels.

Herb Bush waved from across the room. "Rick, we have room at our table." He motioned in front of him. His redheaded wife had the seat beside him, and another older couple occupied two other seats at the table. Rick nodded and strolled in that direction.

"Good to see you here, our young Yankee friend." Herb nodded at an empty chair.

"Nice to see you all, too. This is a good cause, and I figured it was a worthy event to show up for." Rick took a seat next to Herb.

Tamarind stood at the podium on the platform. She smiled at the group and leaned closer to the microphone. "Hello, everyone."

"How ya doin', Tam?" someone shouted from the floor.

"I'm doing wonderful." She smiled but clutched the podium's edge. "Welcome to Starlight and Sweethearts, and I probably don't have to tell you much about why we're here tonight. The Edelweiss Club raises funds for the Wounded Warrior Project, which does so much for so many. Um, you've probably seen the silent auction items, and there's still time to place your bids. If you're like me and received a Secret Sweetheart gift, you can go to the reception table and pick up a card that contains the name of your gift giver. But for now, we'd like to open the buffet sausage supper after a word of prayer from Reverend Franks." Tamarind motioned to an older man sitting at the head table.

Wow. Rick tried not to marvel as they all stood and bowed their heads. People didn't open fund-raisers like this up north with prayer, especially outside any religious setting. He tried not to let his mind wander as the man prayed, but then his stomach rumbled. Herb coughed.

"Amen," said the minister.

Thirty minutes later, Rick took his last bite of german sausage, savoring the spices and seasonings. If he could purchase this by the pound, he'd consider putting it on his menu. Evidently the family only made it once a year from a secret recipe.

"I'm lookin' forward to hearing Billy speak," Herb said. "His story is quite a testimony to how God can change a man, how He takes broken things and makes them better than before."

"Ah, I see." Rick braced himself. *God changing people? Broken things?*

Tamarind took the podium again and spoke into the microphone. "I'm told that dessert is now available, but there's also plenty of time to complete a pledge form while our guest speaker talks to you about his personal journey and the Wounded Warrior Project."

She took a deep breath and paused. "Former Staff Sergeant Billy Tucker is no stranger to Starlight. This is the first time since his injuries three years ago that he's sharing his own story and not telling someone else's. He's come a long way, but I'll let him share with y'all about that. Please welcome Staff Sergeant Billy Tucker." Tamarind stepped back and let Billy approach the podium.

He unfolded a piece of paper and took a deep breath. "About three years ago, my life changed forever. You all know most of the story already. It was a regular morning in Iraq, but we were anywhere but somewhere regular. Our Humvee took an RPG hit. I was riding in back when the grenade struck. I should have been in the front. If I had been"—he swallowed hard—"I wouldn't be here."

The crowded ballroom was utterly silent. Billy cleared his throat. "The explosion killed our driver and our colonel. All I can remember is a searing pain. Shattered my femur, tibia, fibula. Both forearms were ripped up, with some nerve damage. A concussion was the least of my injuries. I grabbed my weapon, somehow fired over toward the building where the insurgents were hiding. I don't remember anything after that, until waking up in a hospital in Germany, with my parents by my bed."

Rick managed to exhale, not realizing he'd been holding his breath. Of course, soldiers were in and out of the news. But this was the first time he'd heard one share a story firsthand. They were a different breed.

A pause hung in the air, and Justine went to Billy's side and held his hand, not saying a word.

"I thought after my surgeries, after coming home, I was okay once I'd healed up. Physically, I was. Mentally, emotionally, spiritually—no. The Wounded Warrior Project helped me return to myself. I'm not the Billy Tucker who left for that final tour in Iraq. But through the project, with God's help, with my family, and finally, with the love of a good woman who's walked some of where I've walked, I'm here. I'm whole. Scarred, but whole. Right now at Tucker Ranch, we have three cottages for recovering soldiers and their families to spend weekends. It's a small way that I can give back to my brothers, and sisters, in arms.

"If you could find it in your hearts to give, I know that it will help others like me find their way back to wholeness." Billy scanned the room. Rick thought he heard a few sniffles but dared not look around. His own eyes burned. He wanted to rub them but forced himself instead to drink a sip of the cool sweet tea that Azalea Bush had brought for him during supper.

Billy folded his notes. "I thought I'd add that it was getting wounded that brought me to the end of myself. We Tuckers are pretty stubborn. My parents raised us to be strong. We had to be, moving from base to base while my father served in the military. In the end, my pride took the worst wounding of all. I wanted to be like my father—go the distance, serve a career. I served less than ten years. I finally understood, in my pain, that God had never left my side. I'd done a good job shutting Him out without realizing it. He healed me, not like magic, but just in time."

He paused, and the papers shook briefly. "I'm not sure why I added that part tonight. Wasn't planning on it. They almost had to shove me up here to talk about myself. Anyway, thank you all again, and God bless." Billy nodded then stepped away. Applause filled the room, and Rick joined in, following the others in standing ovation.

Herb leaned closer. "What he won't tell you about are his two Purple Hearts, his medals of honor. He's one of those soldiers that makes my generation think there's hope for this modern Army."

Rick nodded, the memory of Billy's words ringing in his ears, louder than the applause. *"God healed me, not like magic, but just in time."* But why the suffering? Why not just prevent Billy from being wounded in the first place? His unanswered questions fought against Billy's story.

Once the hubbub died down and Rick took his seat again, he felt like he had a better grip on his emotions. He wrote out a generous pledge donation on one of the table cards distributed by the Edelweiss Club.

He shook off the heavy feeling and went to get some air. That, and to check if he ought to bid on the meal from The Pit. He saw Tamarind standing beside one of the tables. Their eyes met, and she joined him as he walked toward the building's entryway.

"I'm glad you came," she said. "Listen, about that day at Justine and Billy's…"

"It's okay. I'm good with it if you are. It was an impulsive thing."

She nodded. "I agree with you. It's probably best if it doesn't happen again."

He nodded as well. "You're absolutely right. It shouldn't. Friends?" He extended his hand.

"Friends," she said as they shook. "But I'm still not giving you my barbecue recipe."

"I wouldn't dream of asking for it, since mine will

be so much better." He couldn't resist a little jab back at her, along with a wink.

"Ha. Once you get around to it." She quirked a grin at him, her green eyes challenging him. Which reminded him...

"So, about the roses..." He figured he might as well get that covered, too.

"Roses?"

"Two dozen, long-stemmed yellow roses. With a card. Delivered to you. I confirmed it and everything with Gertrude. There's nothing romantic intended with those. I figured you'd enjoy them."

Tamarind shook her head. "I did get some yellow roses, but they weren't from you."

"Mom, how could you?" Tamarind paced the living room, her feet throbbing after she kicked off her pumps. She was going to throw those killer high heels in the trash or donate them to a thrift store. Once she was done talking to her mother, of course.

"He's not right for you." Her mother crossed her arms as she sat on the couch. "You need to be with someone who is good to you, loyal, Christian, someone who knows you."

"But you don't get to decide for me. Rick is only a *friend*, Mom. A friend. As in not a romantic interest." The sound of the statement hurt a little, but it couldn't be helped. "I can't believe you wrote Mike's name on the card, either. He's my employee. And only a friend, too. I don't think of him that way, romantically, at all." She worked at one of the earring backs, stuck on her ear.

"I am trying to protect you."

"Please don't. I know how to watch out for myself."
Really, they'd had this discussion before. Tamarind
should have been suspicious then that her mother was
going to pull some kind of stunt. "Remember, he's going
to leave, eventually. So try to remember that, and be
happy."

"All right." Her mother frowned. "I think Mike is a
nice young man. You should give him a chance."

"He's my employee, and I've known him forever."
Tamarind shook her head. "I can't see anything happening between us other than a good friendship. He's
a terrific worker."

"Have you ever given him a chance?"

"No, I haven't." Tamarind's phone started ringing
from her handbag. "That's the restaurant. Why would
they be calling so late? They should be shut down by
now."

She pulled out her phone and answered. "This is
Tamarind."

"I think you need to come down here," said Mike.
"I think someone was trying to break into the back of
the store."

"Call the police, and I'll meet you there in five minutes." Tamarind ended the call and went to find her
flats.

# Chapter 10

"What happened?" Tamarind glanced from Mike to the back door of the restaurant, a heavy contraption with a dead bolt and an alarm.

"I was shutting down tonight, getting the bank bag ready with the deposit so you wouldn't have to do it on Monday morning, and I heard something at the back door." Mike held up both hands. "So I went to check, and I could hardly push the door open. I heard a couple of voices and people running. Then I opened the door and found this."

She followed the line of his pointing finger to see fresh heavy gouges in the wood, close to the edge of the door's lock. "The police should be here by now. Did you call them?"

"No, I figured…" Mike scowled.

"I need this documented. That's why I asked you to call them." Her words came out a little more harshly than she intended. "Sorry. I mean, I want the police to see this in case it happens again." She yanked her phone from her purse and dialed.

Within six minutes, a single black-and-white squad car arrived, and Mike's scowl had grown deeper. An officer approached. "I'm Officer Danny Austin with the Starlight Police Department. I'm here about an attempted break-in, and I need to see some ID from both of you."

Tamarind and Mike gave the officer their driver's licenses. "Mike was closing down for the night. He's my manager, and I was at an event at the civic center."

"Yes, someone tried to break in while I was here." Mike pointed at the door. "Looks like they tried to pry it open. Or something."

The officer studied the raw edges of the door. "Maybe a crowbar. I haven't heard of any break-ins recently, but I'll make a note of this and alert our criminal investigations division."

"You don't dust for prints or anything?" Tamarind asked.

The officer shook his head. "Not unless there was an actual forced entry, breaking and entering."

"Well, they probably used gloves," Mike said. "The only prints on the back door would be yours or mine, or the delivery drivers."

"That's true." Tamarind had never felt like she needed to look over her shoulder in Starlight. She pulled her handbag, which contained her small pistol, closer to her. She never wanted to shoot anyone. She'd rather let them take what they wanted, unless they were trying to hurt someone else.

"Don't worry," said the officer. "We'll send a few extra patrols by over the next several days, just cut behind your restaurant to the back street. If someone's watching, then they'll know we are, too. Now, Mike, make sure Ms. Brown gets home safely."

"Of course I will," Mike said.

"Thanks for coming," Tamarind called after the officer as he left. She turned to Mike. "You don't have to follow me home. But I want to look around inside before I go."

Mike nodded. "It was weird. I almost didn't hear them."

She nodded as she entered the rear of the restaurant. The cleanup sink stood opposite the walk-in, and beyond that, the door to the barbecue pit itself, and the office. "Did you have the bank bag ready, you said? Because I'll take that tonight."

"Now I'm definitely going to follow you home."

"You don't have to." She paused. "Look, I need to tell you something...not about the door."

"What is it?"

"Well, I probably shouldn't have said anything a couple of weeks ago when I got those roses, but I thought they were from you." There. At least it was out now.

"I was wondering what you were talking about." He rubbed his forehead. "No, they weren't from me. I... Oh, never mind."

"What is it?"

"I...I would have bought you at least four dozen, if I could."

Tamarind tried not to look surprised. "Oh, Mike. That's a sweet thing to say."

"You're my friend and my boss, but..." Mike shrugged. "Anyway, I can't afford it, though. That's why I was so surprised. I thought you were joking, for some reason."

"The joke was actually on me." Hopefully she could live without any more interference from her well-meaning mother. "You go on ahead. I'll get the deposit bag."

"I'll wait outside in my car until I see you leave."

Tamarind went to the office and took a deep breath. Mike... Her niggling suspicion was confirmed. She hoped any awkwardness between them would go away in time. She pulled out the cloth bank bag, filled with cash and the deposit slip. She'd verify the account at home before stopping at the bank on Monday.

*Someone watching the restaurant?* As Tamarind turned out the light and locked both locks on the back door, she heard a crunch of tires on the gravel for the back lot. *Dad.*

He parked and met her at her car, giving a wave to Mike, who waited inside his car, headlights on, engine running. "Baby girl, what on earth is going on? Your mother said you got a phone call and something about the police. And you weren't answering your phone...."

"Mike thought someone was trying to break in, so I met him down here, and we called the police to check it out."

"I don't like it, don't like it one bit." Her dad shook his head. "Starting Monday, I'm coming out of retirement for a few days each week."

"Dad, you don't have to—"

"Ut-ut-ut." He held up his hand. "If I talked to your friend Rick, he'd agree with me that I have a stake in this restaurant by giving you the down payment. I want to help protect my investment. If that means being here a few nights a week, I don't mind."

"Okay." Tamarind sighed.

"That's it? Okay? I thought you'd put up more of a fuss."

"No, you're right. You could double as my bouncer." She smiled at her father.

"Very funny, baby girl."

Tamarind watched as Mike pulled out of his parking spot, waved at them, then drove off. "Seriously, if anyone thinks of getting rowdy or causing trouble, you can ask them to leave. You can be my bouncer."

Her dad let loose with one of his deep belly laughs. "As if you can't do that yourself. Well, sure. I'm your father. I like to watch out for you. If you need a hand with cooking, you know you can call on me. I don't even have to be on the payroll."

"Oh, Dad. Thanks." She threw her arms around him. "I appreciate everything you and Mom have done for me."

"I know you do, and we're proud of you, too." He looked thoughtful. "I've sort of been missing the old cooking routine, you know. I just don't want to overstep and try to take over. Because this is your dream."

"My kitchen is your kitchen." Maybe he could help her find the discrepancy between the meat bill and the actual meals prepared.

"What is it?"

"I've had a problem with food costs skyrocketing, and I wasn't going to say anything to you. Costs are up, and we don't seem any busier than usual. But we keep running out of inventory."

"Huh. Sounds like a portion control issue to me." He patted her shoulder. "We'll figure it out. That's what families are for, sticking together."

"Thanks, Dad."

"Now let's go home before your mother calls the police to see where we are."

At that, Tamarind had to laugh.

Rick blinked at the bright lights as he entered The Pit on Thursday morning. 6:10 a.m. He thought that should be a moment for the record books. The last time he'd been up at this hour was… Well, he was probably heading home after being out all night. He'd put those days behind him, but evidently dragging himself out of bed still didn't come easier.

"Looky who we have here," Herb said as Rick stifled a yawn and stopped at his table. "Got a chair right here. I tell ya, when I was your age…"

"You were up at four every morning and made sure at least a hundred men were, too. I bet you were insufferable and cheerful." Rick sat down and nodded at another man at the table, a worn, brown leather Bible next to his glass of orange juice. Suzie, the waitress, appeared at his side with a steaming cup of coffee, and he hadn't even ordered any. Now that was service.

"Oh," Herb said. "Where are my manners? This is Ray Holley, with the Exchange Club."

"Yes," Rick nodded at the gentleman. "We met at the fund-raiser on Saturday night."

"That's right." Ray returned the nod. "You're the

one opening the new restaurant in the spring, at the old Millicent House."

"I'm shooting for the first week of May. Slow going."

"Who are you using for a general contractor?"

"Todd Clark."

"Ah." Ray took a sip of his coffee and said nothing more but gave a quick glance to Herb.

"Is that a bad 'ah' or a good 'ah'?" asked Rick.

"Well, Todd's a good guy but not terribly fast. Contractors aren't known for their speed, generally. I'd recommend you stay on him. So you came to town for the restaurant. Got any business or restaurant experience?"

"My business partner and I own and operate two restaurants in New York."

Ray nodded. "Okay, I knew I heard an accent. I'm from Jersey City, originally."

No wonder the guy didn't have much of a twang. "How about that? That's where my parents live."

"Small world. I got here because of Uncle Sam. The wife and I raised our kids and decided to stay in Texas because we didn't want to go back to shoveling snow. We kind of miss four seasons, though."

"Hear, hear," said Herb, raising his coffee cup. "Well, I'm glad our young friend could join us today, although truthfully, I'm sure he'd rather be reading the backs of his eyelids." At that, they chuckled.

"Now, it's not so bad." Rick swallowed some coffee.

"Be honest, though, you're humoring me."

"Well, uh… I'd like to hear what you have to say."

Ray burst out laughing. "That gives us open license to keep you here all day, because we never run out of anything to talk about, do we? And if the others were here, you might as well end up ordering from the supper menu."

Herb said, "We'd rather hear what you have to say, actually, since you disciplined yourself enough to haul yourself out of bed and get down here." Then he waved his hand in Rick's line of vision. "Hello?"

"Oh, sorry, I was a little distracted for a second there." He'd been scanning the other end of the restaurant, seeing if Tamarind was at work this morning. He hadn't seen her since the Starlight and Sweethearts night, when they figured out the misunderstanding about the roses. Gertrude Jenkins didn't have an explanation for what happened with the Secret Sweetheart card, but he would bet that Tamarind would get to the bottom of it.

"Tamarind's busier than a termite in a sawmill," said Herb. "But I bet she'll come out if she knows you're here."

"I noticed that Cleo's working nights now," said Ray. "Bets and I had supper here on Monday."

"Why is her father working nights? Isn't he retired?" Rick asked, ignoring Herb's remark.

"Someone was trying to break in the back door on Saturday night." Herb looked somber, his earlier jovial tone gone. "Can't imagine that around here. Still, there's all kinds in every town."

Rick made a mental note to add security system and cameras to the ever-expanding restaurant budget for Millicent House. "I can't see someone trying to mess with Cleo."

"No, we can't either."

"I'd better get that order in." Ray studied his menu.

"But, anyway. Back to you, Mr. Rick. We study the Bible here, talk about what it means to us, and try to answer one another's questions. Like I said, we could tell you a whole lotta stuff that you probably don't want to know about...right now."

"Ah, yes. Probably." He wasn't used to this honesty, especially about spiritual things. He was more accustomed to either someone trying to sell him something or tell him about the scalding fires of hell. Or both. "I, uh... I'm not sure where to start."

"So you believe in God?" asked Ray.

"I...I dunno. I had it drilled into me from an early age. Catechism, and all."

"Me, too." Ray sighed. "And when I was a kid, Mass was in Latin. What a disconnect."

"Well, what I've seen from some people around here is a little different. You make me want to believe. But the 'Holy Church'"—Rick made quotation marks in the air—"has done evil for the sake of 'God' over the centuries. Why do I want to be a part of that? It's no different now with the big-shot hypocrites of our times." He was ready for the arguments. He'd had Bible thumpers come by his New Jersey apartment, waking him out of a sound sleep on some Saturday mornings, trying to convince him of his eternal "lost" state and certain future damnation.

"You're right," Herb said. "I agree with you."

"You do?"

"I don't blame you one bit for looking at the Church through the ages as being a poor example of Christ." Herb nodded. "It's shameful, really. The Jesus that I read about in the Bible caused an uproar wherever He went, but in a good way. Yes, He confronted sin. That's why He came to earth. Ah, but here I go again, motorin' on."

"I'd venture to say that there have been just as many great examples for Christ as not," said Ray. "If not more. It's easy to look at the bad when there aren't many people who try to live as He wants them to."

"Yes, but…" Rick's phone vibrated on his belt. "One moment, please. That might be Todd, or my mother. My dad's recovering from a heart attack, and I told her to call me immediately if she needs me."

No, it wasn't Todd, or Mom, but Kevin.

"Hey, did you forget about the time difference?" Rick asked.

"I didn't. We've had over eight inches of snow since last night, on top of sleet…. The roof on Pasta-Pasta partially caved in."

"You've got to be kidding me." Rick frowned. The other men at the table shot him questioning glances. "I'll get there as soon as possible."

"LaGuardia and JFK are shut down," Kevin said. "There's nothing you can do for the moment."

"We'll have customers and employees who'll want to know what to do." Rick felt the beginnings of a headache prick his forehead.

"We're closed, of course. Wait till the airports open, then get up here."

"You can count on it." Rick ended the call. "There's a bad snowstorm in the Northeast, and part of the roof has caved in at one of my restaurants. I'll have to go back to New Jersey sooner than I planned."

"God sees and knows," said Herb. "We'll pray about it."

"That's another thing...." Rick set his phone on the table. "Why doesn't God prevent things like this from happening? I mean, I'm no saint, so this doesn't surprise me that the roof's caved in. But my father, he's one of the good guys. Devout. A good husband. The best father, the best friend anyone could ask for. But he had a heart attack. He's not back on his feet yet. I want him around for..." He almost said *for when I finally have a family* but stopped.

"Prayer isn't a good-luck charm," Ray interjected. "I can't explain how God works through our prayers. I know we're to represent Him on the earth.... You know in the Lord's Prayer, 'Thy will be done, on earth as it is in heaven.' We're asking for what God wants for the situation."

"But...people pray all the time and things don't turn out the way they ask." Rick tried not to raise his voice. He wasn't arguing, just...confused.

"Sometimes only God knows why we don't get what we ask," said Herb. "You know, I still wake up in the middle of the night sometimes, thinking I'm somewhere in 'Nam, kicking and fighting the bedsheets, scarin' Zalea out of her good night's sleep. I went through that mess over forty years ago, so you'd think it would leave me alone once and for all. At one time, I begged God to please take the nightmares away from me. Finally I quit struggling and begging when it didn't happen. Maybe God wants me to remember. Maybe some soldier who's done four or five tours in Iraq comes through that door, and he's questioning everything he ever knew or believed. I can tell him with certainty, I know what he's facin', because I've been there, too."

Rick nodded. He'd never thought of it that way before. "Well, I guess it'd be a good thing to pray about my trip north. I can't be up there too long, not while trying to keep an eye on things here. I have so much to do…a design team from the college to supervise, a menu to plan, employees to hire, and then there's marketing."

"We can pray about all of those details," said Herb. "The very hairs of your head are numbered, Rick Mantovani."

"What does that mean?" Rick asked.

"It's from the Bible," Ray answered. "Do you have a Bible?"

"Uh, no."

Ray reached under the table for his briefcase and opened it. He pulled out a brand-new Bible. "Here. This is for you. I always keep one on hand in case I get a chance to give it away."

Rick's collar tightened. They were sucking him in, with all their talk about prayer and Bibles and God. But he'd brought it up first, and now everything had snowballed into a spiritual avalanche. "Uh, thank you."

"This isn't a Catholic Bible, just so you know," Ray said. "You should probably start with the book of John. Any of his books are great. They're my favorites."

Rick didn't recall promising he'd read it, but he accepted the gift. "I appreciate the tip."

"Hey, you have a Bible," Tamarind said as she ambled up to the table. She looked awfully fresh and pretty for the morning hour. Rick was still pushing the sand out of his brain.

"Uh, Ray just gave it to me."

The other two men were nodding, glancing from Tamarind to Rick, then back to Tamarind again. They grinned like two little boys with their hands in the cookie jar, spreading the joy around.

"That's neat." She gave him a hesitant smile, not like her usual confident grin.

"Can I talk to you for a moment?" he asked her.

"Sure. In my office?"

He nodded. "Gentlemen, this'll only take a moment."

"Take whatever time you need; we'll be here. Just drinking our coffee."

Rick zigzagged through the tables behind Tamarind, past the service counter and down the hallway to her office.

"What's up?" she asked as they entered the space. It reminded him of his office. No one spent any time there, but somehow the paperwork grew.

"I'm going back to New York, probably first thing in the morning."

"Is it your dad?" She laid her hand on his arm, her eyes narrowing in a concerned squint.

"No." He explained about the restaurant. "That's why I need your help. I know you're busy, but I have full confidence in you."

"What for? I mean, I'll help out if I can...."

"If you could keep me posted on what the contractor's doing? He's had to rewire the whole place, not just the kitchen, to get it up to code, which set us back on our schedule. I have everything in a folder." He raked his hand through his hair. "Just swing by and see what's going on. I'll give you my plans and an extra key."

"I'll do my best." She smiled at him, and in a flicker of memory he saw her in that amazing red dress from Saturday night.

"Uh, did you ever find out what happened about the roses?" He had to ask.

Tamarind glanced over his shoulder then back at him. "My mother. She saw the order come in and changed the name card." Her cheeks bloomed a shade of rose. "I'm embarrassed."

"Don't be. It wasn't your fault." He wanted to say more, but what would be the point? His place was really in New Jersey, this latest event reminded him. This was the trouble being so far away from home.

"She lied, Rick. She interfered, and she shouldn't have." Tamarind frowned. "Well, you keep me posted on how things are going in New York, and I'll tell you how everything's going here."

"Deal." He smiled at her. "When I get back, I'll owe you dinner."

"I'll hold you to that."

Her smile would follow him all the way back to New York.

# Chapter 11

"Do you have Skype?" Rick asked. His voice came through the speakerphone as Tamarind sat at her desk in the office, trying to work on the eternal paperwork nearly two weeks later.

"No, but I can probably download it on my laptop."

"It would be easier than the phone, and wouldn't use our cell phone minutes."

Her dad was bustling around the kitchen outside, and he stopped long enough to say, "Tell that Rick he needs to get himself back here."

"Dad says he misses you, sends hugs your way," she said.

"Ha, right. I heard him." Rick chuckled. "What a mess up here. I'm trying not to lose sleep at night, but the insurance company is taking forever at approving our contractor's estimate. That, and it's costing me—or us—money every day that we're closed."

"Do you know how long it'll take before you re-open?"

"I'm not sure. Kevin—my business partner—has already found someone to do the repairs. But then we need the health department to inspect…"

"Is that something you have to be up there for?"

"No, but this is my place. I'm responsible for it. So, is everything okay with Millicent House?"

"Yes, it's going great. The rewiring's done. They're installing the extra bathroom, and the drywall is up everywhere else." She didn't want to admit the real reason she was wondering when he'd return.

"So it's going well, then."

"Yes…"

"I know why you're asking why I have to be up here. You miss me, don't you?" He chuckled. "That's why you're pining for my return."

"Why would I be pining?" She couldn't keep the grin from stretching across her face. "You're in the place you call home. Texas is just a temporary exile for you."

"You're right.… I am home. But I have a responsibility down in Texas, and I can't forget it either."

"Of course you won't. So, when are you coming back?"

"I wish I could tell you. Another week, maybe?"

"Okay. Did you get the links to the paint colors I e-mailed?"

"I did. I like the sandstone best. And the painter?"

"Will be ready to go after the drywall is done."

"Excellent. I knew I could count on you."

"I'll be glad when you're here to take over," Tamarind said.

"Me too, me too." A pause hung between them. "You know why I asked about Skype?"

"Why's that?"

"Because I miss seeing your face." His tone went lower.

Her heart did a little flip-flop. "Well, I miss being seen."

Rick cleared his throat. "I, uh... By the way, I've been reading the Bible that Ray gave me. He recommended a few books for me to start out with."

Her heart warmed. "You have?"

"I've read them a few times over. Interesting... I don't exactly get all of them. John can be a little obscure, but I thought you'd like to know."

"Well yes, I'm glad you told me. I think that's terrific."

"You almost done, Tam?" Her father's voice made her jerk upright in the chair. "Because someone from the Starlight Police Department is here to talk to you."

"Sure, Dad. I'll be right there."

"Guess you need to go?" Rick asked.

"Yes."

"I'll call you this weekend."

"I'll download Skype."

"Awesome. We'll talk more then...face-to-face."

Tamarind hurried to the front of the restaurant to see a tall, slim woman with wavy blond hair pulled back into a neat ponytail. She had a badge clipped to one hip, and she wore a sidearm on the opposite side.

"I'm Tamarind Brown," she said to the detective at the counter.

"Detective Megan James," said the blond. "I understand you reported someone possibly trying to break into the back of your restaurant a couple of weeks ago."

"Yes, my night cook, Mike, said he heard someone at the door when he was closing down for the evening. It sounded like they were trying to break in. So I asked the police to send someone. We found some gouges on the door, as if someone was trying to use a crowbar on it or something."

The detective placed a manila folder on the counter and opened it. "We have some still photos here, pulled from video recorded by the bank's security cameras next door. The reason we ended up with the camera footage is that someone has been vandalizing the drive-through machines. However, the cameras happened to catch something, or someone, behind your restaurant that same night."

Tamarind studied the photos. "This shot looks pretty far off." A photo taken across the bank parking lot, with the rear of The Pit in full view. A figure, holding a slim narrow object, curved at one end. The shot was dated the Saturday night of the Starlight and Sweethearts event.

"Yes, but we have a few close-up still frames." The detective motioned. "Do you recognize this person at all?"

Tamarind looked closer at the enlarged still photo. A familiar-looking man, wearing blue jeans and a T-shirt, using a crowbar to pull at the back door.

*Mike.*

"Did the snowblower cooperate?" his mother asked as Rick entered the warm kitchen, stomping his feet on the inside doormat.

"Yes and no." He pulled his feet out of his boots then peeled off his gloves and put them on the counter. "That's a very wet snow. I hope it's the last storm of the season."

"Oh, I hope it's not ruining the work on your restaurant."

"No, it's not. They have tarps over the new framework and will be putting up the new roof as soon as the weather clears." He took off his wool jacket. "I bet it's a lot warmer in Texas right now."

"All this back and forth, back and forth from Texas. It must be costing you a fortune."

"It's not bad." He helped himself to a cup of coffee from the coffeepot.

One more day, and he'd be flying back to Texas. Tamarind assured him that the main dining area was ready to go, except for the furniture installation and accessories, and the kitchen extension was full speed ahead with a projected completion date by the end of March, in a little more than two weeks. He'd return to Starlight and begin conducting job interviews. He needed a manager and a chef who could handle the menu. He had leads from a friend who ran an Austin restaurant. If anything, he might be able to open mid-April.

His mother spoke again. "I don't know if I told you or not, but Jessica Pignetti and her husband just had their third baby."

"Pignetti?"

"Oh, you knew her as Jessica Florentino. Remember her? You dated a few times."

"Okay, now I remember. Sort of." She had demanded

he choose between his restaurant and her. Mantovani's was his pride and joy, his baby, and he was flush with the glee of his first restaurant at the young age of twenty-three. She told him to stick to a forty-hour workweek or forget being with her. He didn't blame her walking out of his life.

"That could have been you. She adored you." His mother's tone was chiding.

"I know she did. But I couldn't just drop the restaurant. She knew what it meant, the long hours. I had to be there. I never led her to believe otherwise."

"Instead of two grandchildren from you, I have a third restaurant on the way."

"Ma!" Good grief. He shook his head.

"Well, it's true. You're going to be thirty-three years old, and you have three restaurants. How are they going to take care of you when you're older?"

"I'm not older. Not yet." Here they went again. It usually happened, the more time he spent with his parents, especially his mother. She meant well. But he'd settle down when the time was right, and the right woman wouldn't demand he choose one or the other. In fact, for the right woman, he'd gladly slow down if she didn't pressure him.

"Did those snowdrifts eat you up out there?" His father's voice boomed from the front room.

"Nope, not exactly."

"Go on." His mother shooed him in the direction of the living room. "Go keep your father company. I can tell you don't want to listen to me, and after all, you're leaving tomorrow anyway."

"Aw, Ma," he began, but she waved him away. She'd

bring the same topic up again in the future. He could guarantee it. Plus, her efforts seemed intensified now, since it wasn't a holiday or other family gathering but him simply helping out around their house. He trudged to the living room, pausing long enough to drape his coat on the rack in the front hallway.

"Can't believe you're leaving again, so soon," his father said as he entered the room. TV Land was playing yet another ancient Western.

"I need to get back." Rick sank onto the couch, its springs complaining. He knew what gift to give them for Christmas, months and months away. But they didn't mesh well with change. A leather sectional would *not* be their item of choice.

"So, you want to talk to your pop."

"I'm just spending the day with you guys before I leave again."

"Ha. You got something on your mind."

Rick wasn't sure where to begin, so he started with the first question that came into his mind. "Do you love God, Dad?"

"What kind of question is that? I'm a Catholic, I'm part of the Church. Don't let your mother hear you. I'm sure she'd be happy if you went to a Catholic church in Texas. They do have them, don't they?"

"Yes, Dad. Starlight has one."

"Just one?"

"But that's not what I'm talking about. Have you ever read the Bible?"

"What? I don't know. I read the missal with the scripture readings." His dad's brow furrowed. "Ricky, I don't understand where these questions are coming from. What's happening to you?"

"I'm not sure, Dad."

"You're not joining a cult and shaving your head or anything, are you?"

"No, not at all." He almost laughed.

"Well, good." Dad huffed a sigh. "Look. I go to Mass, I go to confession. I pray. I try to do what's right. Why are you asking me all these questions?"

"Someone gave me a Bible when I was in Texas, and I started reading it. An older man gave it to me. He's about your age. He suggested that I read books written by the apostle John. So I did. In one of them it says that God is love, and how if we confess our sins, He will cleanse us." He felt like he was starting to see something he'd never realized before, as if something far off was coming into focus with a high-powered lens.

"Yes, God is love. We should go to confession, get our absolution, and then do our penance."

Rick nodded. That's what he figured his father might say. He wasn't sure what he was hoping to hear. He'd had the idea of sin hammered into him since before his First Communion. Sin, in child-sized lessons. Part of him didn't want to read John's words about sin—that if someone said they didn't sin, they were liars. Part of him knew, though, the stories of God's holiness. He shook off the thoughts. They'd have to wait for Texas.

After a supper of Mantovani-like portions, Rick headed back for his apartment. He still needed to pack, and his flight headed out of LaGuardia for Dallas at 8 a.m. However, he would gain an hour by flying southwest to Texas. Around ten he decided to call Tamarind, since his thoughts wouldn't quit.

"You're up late for an early flight," she said.

"I know. I can't sleep. Plus, I figure I'm getting my hour back tomorrow."

"So what's up?"

"Can't I just call you to say hi?"

"You rarely 'just call' me. Not that there's a problem with that, of course."

"I was thinking about something I saw you write in a note, my first Sunday at church down there."

"What was that?"

"You wrote something like *I can't do anything to make God love me more than He does right now.*"

"Oh, I did?"

"Yes. The first part sounds like something I read in one of the John books. But what do you mean about the second part?"

"Well, I was trying to remind myself that God's love isn't earned. He *is* love, so we don't do anything to deserve it. That's His nature."

"But then there's the whole sin thing."

"Right. We're born into a sinful fallen world. I believe that there's a hole inside us that only God can fill. He's the only one that can give us true peace, true forgiveness."

He let her statement hover in the air between them. "Okay. Well, thanks for explaining that to me." He knew about original sin, but he'd cast the notion aside with everything else to do with religion.

"No problem. I'm glad you're reading that Bible."

"I guess I just want to know for myself, because you

and Herb and of course the pastor at church have given me a lot of things to think about."

"I wanted to tell you something, too. I was going to wait until you got back to tell you, but Mike's gone."

"What? Did he quit?"

"No. I fired him. Turns out he was the one trying to make it look like someone was breaking into the restaurant, to throw me off from suspecting one of my employees was stealing. Suzie confessed to me that she'd seen him leave with a whole brisket on more than one occasion. She said he told her that I told him he could have it, since I couldn't raise his salary. He's been doing it for months. Only part of that was true. I couldn't afford to pay him more. I can only imagine how much meat he lifted that Suzie didn't notice."

"That's tough.... Did he get arrested?"

"No. There's no proof that he stole anything. His word against Suzie's. The police detective actually brought photos of him gouging the back door. So, I fired him for that. Lost a friend, too."

"I'm sorry. I know that must have been hard for you. But necessary."

"I never would have imagined him stealing. Helping himself like that. And then lying." She huffed out a sigh. "You were right, Rick. I have to admit it."

"We'll print that statement out and frame it." He grinned, then the expression slid from his face. "But seriously though, I've had to fire a few employees over the years. I don't like it. Sometimes it's easy in certain cases. You know what?"

"What's that?"

"We'll continue this conversation tomorrow night, once I'm back in Texas. Dinner's on me."

## Chapter 12

"Here we are." Rick opened the door to Rebecca's Kitchen with a flourish. "I heard this place has great pie."

"It does," Tamarind said as she entered the small log-cabin restaurant in Kempner, just outside of Starlight. "I haven't been here in a while." This wasn't a date, she reminded herself. They were two friends touching base after being separated while working on a project. *His* project that had claimed much of her time. With Dad stepping in at The Pit, especially now that Mike was out of the picture, her workload had lightened some. She pushed aside the guilt at the idea of her father having to work.

"Where do you want to sit?" He gestured to the weathered booths then to a neat little table for two by the front window. The view overlooked the country highway and a cattle pasture across the road.

"I'll take the table for two by the window. I'm not a big fan of booths, personally."

"After you, then." He shook his head. "I had no idea you can't stand booths."

"If I could remove the ones at The Pit, I would, and change them out with tables. Not in the budget, though." She sat at one end of the little table, and he took the other.

He placed a folder on the table between them. "Maybe it will be, eventually. Had you ever thought of taking on other investors?"

"Not really. My parents helped, of course. And Dad's really outdoing himself now." Tamarind tapped the folder. "What's this?"

"I thought you'd like to see *my* menu, to show you that you have nothing to worry about when Millicent House opens."

She picked up the folder, emblazoned with a line drawing of a building that looked an awfully lot like Millicent House. "So you're sticking with Millicent House, then, and not Rick's Fabulous Western Barbecue anymore?"

"Nope." He shook his head. "Every time I called someone like a contractor or delivery person, I'd have to explain it was at the old Millicent place. So it's stuck— Millicent House. I'm not going to fight it anymore."

"Well, I like the name. It fits the area and shows you're not trying to change things too much. A lot of the old-timers probably have a hard time with that. Sometimes change really freaks them out." She opened the folder.

"I hope they don't mind the menu too much."

Tamarind scanned the mock-up menu page. *Fresh dill cucumber salad; daikon radish salad; shredded carrot salad over butter lettuce, topped with vinegar and olive oil; fingerling potato salad with green chile and cilantro salsa; pear salad with caramelized pecans.*

She wasn't sure about the radish salad, but the pear salad sounded yummy. Then for the sides: *Gourmet mac 'n' cheese, squash casserole, baked potato casserole, sweet potato fries, oven-roasted broccoli with pecans and brown butter, german potato salad.* Lots of carbs. Some customers would like that. Plus, the squash casserole sounded healthy enough, as did the broccoli. Maybe she should change up her own menu. His bread selection scored major points with a list of cheddar bacon corn muffins, whole-wheat bread, and gluten-free loaf.

The proteins for the main dishes gave her pause. *Grilled smoked salmon chunks, smoked alligator, elk barbecue, venison stew with chanterelle mushrooms and pearl onions, top-cut beef barbecue, pulled pork wrapped in puff pastry, barbecued tofu and apples. Tofu?*

"What do you think?"

"Barbecued tofu?" She giggled in spite of her effort to keep her expression even and her voice quiet. "I think the alligator and salmon are a nice touch, but tofu?"

"You'd be surprised."

"Well, you're definitely not competing against me, in a manner of speaking."

"Sorry for the wait." A brunette with short dark hair and a white apron stopped at their table. "What can I get you to drink?"

"Sweet tea for me," said Tamarind. "I'd also like your

chicken-fried steak with baked potato, broccoli casserole, and oil and vinegar for my salad."

"Coffee, plus ice water," said Rick. "And I'll order the same thing that she's having."

"You got it. I'll be right back with your drinks." The lady left and headed toward the kitchen.

"So, the menu layouts have been sent to the printer, linens ordered, plates, glasses, flatware. The kitchen is going in either late this week or early next." Rick grinned. "I was able to order a lot of supplies online while I was in New York."

"You look like you're ready to give yourself a pat on the back." With that look on his face, he appeared ready to conquer the world.

"Maybe, just a little. Everything's come together better than I hoped it would, even with the ice storm delaying us a couple of days and the slow contractor."

She nodded. "Now what?"

"I should have insisted on taking you to dinner in Austin, to thank you properly for helping keep an eye on things while I was gone. Dinner here just doesn't seem enough to me."

"This is perfect. I like supporting local businesses."

"Does she cut into your clientele at all?"

"Not really. Our menus are different, and she specializes in dessert, especially her pie and cheesecake." Tamarind took in the sight of Rick, scanning the restaurant and studying the laminated menu. She could see his mind working, suggestions he'd make, assessing aspects of the restaurant he liked. Rick was definitely a visionary. She liked that about him. She liked a lot about him.

"So," Rick said as he pulled the folder out of her hands and closed it. "Enough restaurant talk. How are your parents?"

"Fine. Mom's really sorry about the flowers. But she's proud. I don't know if she'll say anything to you about it. Dad has hit his second wind, working at the restaurant. I used to wonder when he and Mom helped me buy it, if he was trying to recapture what his father had in Kansas City." She sipped her sweet tea. A late March breeze drifted into the window. Spring. She smiled at Rick.

"So why didn't your parents move back to Kansas City after he retired?"

"Their roots are here. Starlight's their home." Tamarind shrugged. "Most people either love it or hate it around here, near Fort Hood. You don't get much indifference."

"Well, I like it."

"Let me know again how you like it in July." She grinned at him. "You haven't experienced summer in central Texas yet."

"We were up near Dallas at a competition last July, remember?" Rick looked up as their server returned with two plates of food. "I vividly remember the heat then."

"That seems like a long time ago, doesn't it?" Tamarind couldn't believe how much had changed in eight months.

"A lot has happened...." He nodded and looked down at the chicken-fried steak in front of him, smothered with country gravy and sided by a foil-wrapped baked potato. A little dish held a generous chunk of broccoli casserole.

"You're right." When she'd first met the dark-haired, Italian guy from New Jersey last June, she thought he was just another wannabe, and she'd show him how to do barbecue the right way. She figured he would head back to New Jersey with those gorgeous brown eyes of his, and she'd never see him again. Now those brown eyes were studying her, as if trying to read her thoughts.

"This is certainly a country dinner."

"It's called comfort food for a reason." She waved her fork at him. "Consider yourself comforted."

"Yes, ma'am," Rick responded with a fake drawl that made her giggle. "What else do you do for fun around here, besides work, and shoot guns, and do fund-raising?"

"I thought you weren't planning to stay long."

"I'm not going to be at the restaurant 24-7 once it opens."

"Well, okay then." Tamarind thought for a moment. "There's the lake. That's always nice. And camping. But you don't strike me as much of an outdoors guy."

"I'm not." He grinned at her, his eyes twinkling.

"You know, if you're here long enough into the fall, Dad will try to drag you hunting."

"I'll try to remember that." They talked and ate their way through their meals. Tamarind almost said something about this being the best nondate she'd ever been on but decided against it. She hoped that Rick would cross paths more with Billy and Jake Tucker, since they were all around the same age. But Rick's world was different from theirs. She realized, though, that she wouldn't want him to be any other way.

He placed a quarter on the table in front of her. "A quarter for your thoughts?"

"Isn't that supposed to be a penny?" She touched the coin.

"Your thoughts are worth far more than a mere penny."

"If that's the case, pull out your debit card." They both laughed.

"You were thinking there for a few minutes, far away from here."

"Actually, not so far away. I was thinking about what a remarkable man you are, and how I'm glad you're not anyone other than who you are." She studied her empty plate. The admission made her feel vulnerable. She'd tried so hard to tread carefully and not cross any lines.

"I take that as a high compliment, coming from you." He stared down at his mostly eaten baked potato then up at her again, his brown eyes soft. "Because finally, I have to admit, the main reason I came here was...you."

They'd talked and laughed and stuffed themselves with Rebecca's cherry pie, made from real cherries and not the canned bright-red sugary stuff, topped with ice cream. Tamarind sighed at the memory. He'd dropped her off at home after supper. As much as she longed to enjoy more of the early spring evening with Rick, morning came early for both of them. Plus, their outing was drifting too close to being a date.

"Oh come on, who are you fooling?" Tamarind said

to herself as she sat down at her computer. "It might as well have been a date after all."

Rick had talked an awful lot about his restaurants, but tonight she decided to see for herself. She typed in the information for Mantovani's, and up popped the website. Elegant stately columns, a stunning water feature that ran through the center of the dining room.

She clicked on a link for reviews. *Manhattan's youngest playboy chef takes the island by storm with his reinterpretation of classic Italian cuisine.* The photo had a younger version of Rick in his chef jacket, arms crossed over his chest and a grin cocky enough to be worn by Bobby Flay.

The words *playboy chef* nudged her, and it wasn't a comfortable nudge. Of course, Rick was younger here in this photo. Plus, the article was almost ten years old. People changed, matured. He didn't seem the type now.

Tamarind moved on to the Pasta-Pasta website, its media page recently updated with news of the late-winter storm damage and its reopening a week ago. A recent photo of Rick. He wore his chef jacket and was flanked by two glamorous-looking girls. The caption? *Rick Mantovani, one of Manhattan's hottest young chefs, looks ready to step out on the town as Pasta-Pasta reopens after a late-winter snowstorm.*

Jealousy bit Tamarind hard with its sharp teeth. She clicked on any other link, just to get her off the media page. This is why she'd drawn lines for herself. She'd seen friends compromise and end up in heartbreaking relationships. One girl she'd known in high school married a guy who had attended the church's singles' group just because he wanted to find a wife who wouldn't cheat on him. No matter that he could do what he wanted.

Yes, there were wolves in sheep's clothing in the world. However, Rick had always been honest with her.

She clicked out of the web browser, closed her laptop cover, and bowed her head. "Lord, I know You don't want me to be confused about Rick. But that's how I feel right now. Maybe I shouldn't have surfed around and read up on him. If I need to let him go, so be it. I care for him, though, and that's hard. I don't want a relationship with him if neither of us is ready. Please help us. Make Yourself real to him, as only You can. Thank You...." She felt a little sad at the idea of letting him go.

But for her own heart's sake, she knew it was what she had to do.

## Chapter 13

With the final push to open Millicent House, Rick found himself operating on caffeine and adrenaline. He'd hired six waitstaff out of nearly forty applicants from Starlight. His buddy Mac from Austin had sent him a manager, Franco, two years out of culinary school. Young enough to train, yet not so inexperienced that he couldn't run the place while Rick was up north. Franco also came with an executive chef, Matt, a local boy from Starlight who'd gone to culinary school with Franco.

Opening night came, a Friday night in the middle of April. A perfect evening to have supper out for the citizens of Starlight and the surrounding towns.

"Chef Rick," said Franco. "The writer and photographer from *Texas Monthly* are here."

"Excellent." The *Texas Monthly* piece would run close to the holidays and hopefully give him some foot traffic during that time of year. The local press was coming—the Killeen newspaper as well as the one from nearby Copperas Cove, along with their photographers. The local press would give him immediate exposure.

He'd never get tired of this, unveiling a new restaurant. Kevin had even flown down from New York along with Mom and Dad, although Dad looked a little pale and tired easily. At 6 p.m., Gertrude Jenkins arrived with her entourage from the chamber of commerce, along with the mayor.

"Welcome, everyone," said Gertrude. "We are so happy to welcome Rick Mantovani to Starlight, and we look forward to seeing what he's done with Millicent House."

With that, she handed the ceremonial scissors to Rick, and he cut the ribbon blocking the front entrance. The crowd cheered, and he grinned. The top of the world was a beautiful place indeed.

"Follow me, and we'll begin our supper service." The website and social media pages had listed his menu for weeks, with a few jeers but mostly cheers. However, the dining room's design had been a carefully kept secret.

Rick crossed the refinished and distressed hardwood floors and stood at the edge of the dining room as his hostess, Marie, began seating customers. They commented on the ceiling with its pot lights around the perimeter of the room and rustic-looking lights over each table. Tonight, the air was just chilly enough for a small fire in the renovated fireplace.

He wished Tamarind could see this, but she said they had a big group party at The Pit, and she would need to be there. Was that an excuse? Probably. He'd been busy with the final touches of getting Millicent House ready, and she'd retreated to her own busy schedule as well.

He stepped into the gleaming kitchen and watched the line cooks do their rhythmic dance of getting the food prepared and out to the customers. Tonight's special: everything on the menu, fifty percent off. His marketing plan would have this place firmly in the black by year's end.

"You need to at least go down there," her father was saying. "To congratulate him or check out the competition. Your choice."

"I don't know. I'm not sure if I want to go." Tamarind set the pan of freshly smoked brisket on the prep counter. Man, it sure smelled delicious.

"Oh, of course you do," Suzie said. "I know you've been just dyin' to see the inside of that restaurant. I know I have. No pictures online of it anywhere. Only the outside of the house, all fixed up."

"Maybe I should go." Tamarind bit her lip. "Ever since he's come back here and we had our last, um, meeting about the restaurant, he hasn't needed my help. I haven't heard a peep out of him."

"Go easy on him. He's a busy man," said her father. "I'm sure he'll be happy to see you there."

She went to the hand-washing sink. "Okay, I'm going. I'm going."

"See, now that wasn't so hard, was it?" asked Suzie.

"No…" Tamarind said aloud. But Suzie had no idea what swirled inside Tamarind, not at all. Ever since she'd closed that laptop and prayed about letting Rick go, it had been hard for her.

Maybe they'd let up on her if she at least went to check it out. She put on her jacket and headed down the street. Parking was at a premium, especially tonight. Lights glowed in all the windows of Millicent House.

She finally found a parking spot and headed for the entrance. Once inside, she stopped. Stared. Tried not to let the people behind her run into her. *Magnificent* was the first word that came to mind when she saw the dining room.

*Grungy* was the first word that came to mind when she compared her place to this.

"Would you like a seat?" the hostess was saying to her. "It'll be at least a forty-five-minute wait at this point."

Tamarind almost said no but then, "Yes, I would. The name's Brown."

"You can have a seat here in our waiting area or outside on the side patio. Take your pick."

"Thanks, I'll sit inside." Tamarind managed to find one edge of a cushion on the banquette seating along the wall. She scanned the dining room. Not terribly big. In fact, she was certain that The Pit had room for twenty more customers than this place.

The crowd was murmuring, the happy kind of murmur that means good food is heading their way. A keyboard player in the corner was coaxing beautiful music from a baby grand piano. Camera flashes illuminated the relaxed atmosphere.

The words of someone sharing the same banquette cushion caught Tamarind's attention. "It's about time that Starlight gets some quality independent dining establishments. I'm so excited to try this menu. I've been looking forward to it for weeks."

"You and me both. Usually we'd have to go to Austin to get food like this. I might order one of each entrée just to try everything."

"It's certainly going to outshine that hole in the wall down the street."

"Is that what it's called, Hole in the Wall? I thought it was called The Pit."

"Pit, hole. Same difference. This place puts it to shame already."

Tamarind's cheeks blazed. Is this what people thought about her place? She was sorely tempted to get up and walk out right then, and retreat to The Pit to lick her wounds and contemplate minimizing damages. Because Millicent House had the potential to torpedo The Pit. She could see it happening. She'd walked right into it, helping Rick. Perhaps she needed to get a little tougher and use some better business sense. Not to hurt his business, but not go out of her way to help it, as she had been while he was away.

"You're here." Rick stood in front of her as she fought to keep her corner of the banquette seat. "I thought you were busy tonight."

She stood and nearly bumped into him as she did so. He wore his chef jacket and the confidence to go with it. "Yes, I am. But Dad and Suzie convinced me to come."

"So what do you think, now that you see it all put together? I know you saw bits and pieces, but this is the whole thing, at last." Rick beamed as he led her to the dining room floor.

"It's… It's gorgeous. A million times better than my place."

"Apples and oranges, my dear, apples and oranges." He stopped at the limestone fireplace, and she almost ran into him again. "There's no comparison."

"Yes, that's true." Tamarind looked past him, toward the kitchen area. "Shouldn't you be back there?"

"I will be soon enough. I'm letting Matt sweat a little, though." Rick grinned. "It's good to see you. I've been so busy, but I've missed you."

"I…I've missed you, too," she admitted. "Look, I know you're busy, and I should get back to work myself. But I'm glad I came down." *Mostly glad… Partly glad… No, a little regretful.* This way she could say she hadn't been avoiding the place. She wouldn't be coming back here anytime soon, though. The blatant reminder of how her place lacked didn't help her morale.

"I'm glad you did, too." Rick looked as though he was going to say something more, but a crash of metal on tile came from the kitchen. "Gotta run."

And so, he was off.

## Chapter 14

Tamarind smiled up at the sun on the first of May, ignoring the buildup of clouds to the west. *April showers bring May flowers, but Mayflowers bring pilgrims.* She shook her head at the old childhood saying.

April's bluebonnets had come and gone, and Cinco de Mayo was around the corner. Now that Mike was gone from The Pit, things were looking up at last. While food costs were still hard to deal with, her bank account was no longer hemorrhaging. Dad was awesome, especially since his help was free. Suzie was turning into a decent manager trainee. In fact, Tamarind was doing a trial run this morning, meeting Liann to get a pedicure. Her poor feet took enough of a beating, and they deserved a break. So did she.

"You girls are back," Chin Mae said, welcoming them with hugs. The pungent scent of nail polish remover filled the salon.

"Yes. Decided to take the morning off." Thunder cracked outside, and Tamarind glanced to the large front window. Yes, she'd rolled up the windows on her car. Chin Mae would probably make some tea and bend their ears for a good while.

It didn't matter, though. Today, Tamarind felt like a weight had been lifted for good, at least as far as the restaurant was concerned. Now she'd start gaining ground. Already, in just the past few weeks, she'd seen an improvement in her cash flow. She'd been so unwise to blindly trust Mike. Maybe she could start making some renovations to give the interior a facelift. She couldn't afford anything like Rick's renovations at Millicent House, but maybe she could reupholster the booth cushions—or better yet, get rid of the ugly monstrosities.

"You okay?" Liann asked.

"Yes. Or, I will be." Tamarind shrugged. "I didn't ever want to suspect Mike of stealing from me. When Rick suggested one of my own employees was stealing, I didn't believe him." She tried not to punctuate her words with a sigh, but it came out anyway. Now that Millicent House was open, Rick's days in Starlight were numbered.

Hopefully, The Pit's days weren't.

A flash of lightning reflected off the salon's mirrored walls as Chin Mae motioned Tamarind and Liann over to the cushioned pedicure chairs.

"Is it raining yet?" asked Liann.

"Not yet." The parking lot held a yellow glow. Tamarind settled onto the closest chair. "I can get used to this."

"Well, you need to come when you take a morning off. Be good to your feet." Chin Mae shook her head at the sight of Tamarind's toenails.

Tamarind resisted the urge to curl her toes so Chin Mae couldn't see. Good thing she never bothered with manicures in her line of work.

"So, is your man going back to New York soon?"

"I'm sure he is." She wanted to add, *but he's not my man.* She'd wrangled with her feelings for weeks now. Of course she knew the biblical reference to the yoke of oxen. If two unequal oxen were put to work together, they'd end up fighting instead of working in harmony. The Bible talked about spiritual compatibility being vital to a close relationship.

But she and Rick had chemistry. A basic camaraderie brought them together as friends, and somehow things had morphed into something more. But she wasn't going to encourage him. Their past few weeks of distance had been for the best.

However, Rick had a lot of her dad's qualities. Strong, savvy, good for a laugh. Strong enough to stand up to her mother.

"You need to make him stay." Chin Mae started the footbath.

"It's not that simple. There's so much more…." Tamarind wasn't sure how to explain. A rushing sound above them made her look at the drop ceiling.

"The roof." Chin Mae shrugged. "The wind comes, it pulls on the top. I tell the landlord that the back room leaks. He's sending someone out soon. Good thing."

Tamarind willed herself to relax as the rushing noise turned into a rattle. She sank her feet into the warm, soothing footbath. The aroma of tea tree oil tickled her nose. She tried not to think of Rick. She'd told him he was wrong about Mike, when he'd been right all along. She'd acted like a selfish child, reacting as she did when Rick moved into her territory and the focus was pulled from her.

The chimes over the front door sounded, and a whoosh of chilly air blasted into the salon.

Chin Mae glanced toward the reception area. "I'll be right there."

"Looks like a storm's brewin', and it looks like a doozy," came a female voice. Gertrude Jenkins.

Then a low moaning noise rose in pitch. Tamarind sat up straight in the chair. She yanked her feet out of the footbath.

*Tornado siren!*

A siren wailed over the sound of rain pummeling the roof covering the gas pumps. Louder than any police or ambulance wail, the noise made Rick freeze. He was waiting out a hailstorm the size of golf balls that would have damaged his rental car.

"Run!" a voice called out across the parking lot.

"Herb?" Rick swung around to see the older man running toward him, waving his arms as if trying to shoo the storm away. He winced as the hail struck him.

"Tornado…coming…this way." Herb leaned over, panting as he took shelter next to Rick. "We need to get in the drainage ditch. That little convenience store is no match for a storm."

Rick squinted up at the clouds and pouring rain. "I

can't see—" But a roar, louder than any subway he'd ever heard, made the pavement rattle under his feet.

"We can't outrun this. C'mon." Herb was tugging on Rick's sleeve. "The ditch. Runs under the road."

Rick didn't argue with the older man but followed. The rain sliced into them sideways now, the air harder to breathe, as if an invisible vacuum was sucking them backward into the storm.

He wrapped his head partially with one arm as the hailstones struck. Wheezing, panting, Herb lumbered down into the ditch, his shoulders hunched. "Come on. We don't have much time."

Rick barely heard the words. The roar behind them intensified. He cast a glance over his shoulder to see a dark gray mass, wider than a football field, devouring everything in its path. Unseen fingers peeled back the roof of the gas station. His rental car started rocking as if a giant's hand wiggled it side to side.

He followed Herb into the ditch. Herb gestured toward a narrow tunnel under the road.

"Get in."

Rick shook his head. "You first."

The older man gripped Rick by the shoulders and shoved him, scraping his knees, into the drainage ditch. Water stung his eyes as he tried to turn around in the narrow space. He reached for Herb. Wrinkled hands found his. Rick pulled. Something pulled back.

Rick was grasping for pavement. The roar masked his groan. Not Herb.

But Herb was gone.

Rick lay on the concrete spillway. *No. God, no.* He

knew enough about God that you couldn't bargain with Him. All he could do was beg for mercy on Herb.

And Tamarind. Where was she?

The roar overtook his thoughts.

"It's over." Chin Mae's words sounded muffled in Tamarind's shoulder. The older woman sat back on her heels, and tears rolled down her cheeks. "It's over," she repeated. They'd taken shelter in the salon's tiny rest-room, along with Liann and Gertrude, who'd come in to warn them about the storm.

"Is everyone all right?" Tamarind fought to keep her teeth from chattering as she spoke. She rubbed her arms and shivered. A cacophony of thoughts clamored in her ears. *Mom. Dad. Rick. The Pit. Herb. Azalea.* Other names darted through her mind. *Suzie.*

"I'm okay." Liann shifted from her place on the floor next to Tamarind. Gertrude sat huddled in the corner, wedged between the sink and the bathroom door.

"I'm okay, too." Gertrude pulled a phone from her handbag. "I have to call Mitch."

They all shifted to their feet. Liann pushed on the wooden door then rammed it with her shoulder. "Hello? Can anyone hear us?"

"It's not raining anymore…." Chin Mae tipped her head back.

For the first time since they'd slammed the door be-hind them and hunkered down, praying in three lan-guages—Chin Mae in her native Korean, Gertrude in German, and Tamarind and Liann whispering in Eng-lish—Tamarind noticed the roof was gone. Gray clouds drifted above them.

"Something must have fallen against the door." Liann glanced back at them, her hair soaked. Of course, they all were soaked. Tamarind touched her own damp hair, curling into the fierce wiriness inherited from her dad. Her feet were numb. Had her sandals blown away with the roof, or were they tucked neatly next to the cushioned chair she'd been trying to relax on minutes ago?

"Here, we push together." Chin Mae stepped beside her niece. Together, they shoved on the door.

"Okay, it's unlatched." Liann tried to peek out the crack. "It's hard to see the shop."

Tamarind joined them. "Maybe it's a chair or something?" Or the roof, or who knows what else? "Let's try again." She gritted her teeth, and they all pressed. Something on the other side skidded away as the door opened about a foot.

"It's part of the roof," said Liann. She maneuvered through the opening.

Tamarind followed, taking care to watch her step.

She froze where she stood on a clear patch on the tile floor. Daylight illuminated the nail salon. "Oh, Chin Mae... You definitely need a new roof now. And your chairs." She shook her head.

"I can't get a signal. My husband..." said Gertrude, smoothing the sleeves of her light jacket. "He was at our house. Our neighborhood...I can't call." She tiptoed over some boards intermingled with bottles of nail polish.

Chin Mae emerged from the restroom. "Ahhh, it's a mess. A mess." She sank onto a pile of boards and rested her head on her hand. "I don't know...so much to clean up."

Tamarind was at her side. "Don't worry about that right now. Are you hurt at all?"

"No, no. I'm fine." But tears rolled down her cheeks.

"I'm calling Uncle Burt," Liann said.

Tamarind's phone buzzed in her bag, so she pulled it out. Thankfully, it hadn't been squashed when the four of them had piled into the bathroom. "Dad?"

"Baby girl, where are you?" The line crackled.

"At the salon. But I'm okay. We're all right here. The roof is gone."

"We're all right, too. You been by The Pit?"

"No, sir. We just got out of the bathroom here."

"Well, be careful. Is your car all right?"

"I don't know. I can't find my shoes." As if that had anything to do with her car. Maybe she was as bung-fungled as Chin Mae.

"I can come for you if you need me."

"Thanks, Dad. I'll let you know. I need to get to the restaurant."

"I can meet you there. In fact, I'll go now. Let me know if you need a ride."

"I will." She smiled as she ended the call.

"I found one of your sandals." Liann held up Tamarind's slip-on. "Over here under the counter. Tamarind found its mate exactly where she'd left it, next to the cushioned chair, now covered with foam ceiling tiles and metal framing.

Chin Mae sprang to her feet. "Ladies, there will be time to clean up later." She wiped her eyes. "We need to find our loved ones."

*Rick!* Her pulse pounded. Was he at the restaurant? They didn't have storms like this in the Northeast, not usually. Was he able to get somewhere safe? She dialed his number but got a busy signal.

She tucked her phone back into her bag, making sure the ringer was up good and loud, just in case anyone tried to call through.

Tamarind slipped on her sandals then joined the others outside on the sidewalk of Starlight's strip mall, The Plaza—or what was left of it. Looking to the southwest, it appeared as if a devilish finger had traced a line of destruction. Downed trees. Signs, ripped from their poles, blocked Highway 190. A few vehicles sat vacant on the sides of the road.

A few people clustered in a vacant space of the parking lot, so Tamarind headed in their direction. Then she paused. Her car was over by the bank's covered drive-through. Upside down.

Her phone rang. She fumbled for it in her purse. Rick.

"Rick—"

"I'm okay. But your Uncle Herb... I don't know if he's going to make it. We finally got through to EMS, and they're taking him out by helicopter."

## Chapter 15

Rick sank onto the nearest curb, wiping his hands. He'd never seen anything like this, not in his imagining. He wouldn't forget it. The sight of Herb Bush's body, lying in a field beside the parking lot. One of Herb's legs was twisted at an impossible angle, a gash on his head. Finding his own shaky footing to get to him. Begging Herb and whoever else might be listening to just hang on. Hovering over the older man long enough to hear him say in a raspy tone, "The Lord isn't in the wind, Rick.... Listen for His still, small voice...."

Rick sat on the wet ground while Herb lost consciousness. After countless minutes, someone from Starlight Fire Department arrived. The rest was a blur. The EMT offered to check Rick out, but he refused.

"Help Herb. I'm okay." He waved them off and watched the medevac helicopter rise into the sky like a giant metal bird, carrying Herb away with the trauma team.

The convenience store was gone. Leveled, except for the narrow storage closet where the worker and two other customers had hidden. Rick's rental car was now covered with the gas pump awning. If he'd been standing there… He shook his head.

Herb had known what to do while Rick had frozen and stood there, gaping like an imbecile. Herb should have never shoved Rick into that ditch.

Tamarind's comforting words returned to him: *"God has Uncle Herb in His hands. We don't want to lose him, but Herb knows where he's going."* She'd said the words slowly, with only a quaver. Of course no one wanted to lose the old guy. Rick understood why people called the man "Uncle," why he'd become a strong pillar in this town.

*Herb knows where he's going.*

To have that confidence in the face of death…

Then he recalled Herb's words about the still, small voice and God not being in the wind. He didn't know if Herb was being literal or figurative. Rick shook off the thoughts. A cleanup crew would be slow in coming, now that the wrath of the heavens had done its dirty work in Starlight. He headed for the rental car and crawled under the awning. He yanked on the door. Well, he had an online copy of the rental papers somewhere. If the rental was totaled, that was a small inconvenience compared to the devastation carved out by the twister.

He might as well start walking to Millicent House. He hoped there was something left of the place. It was less than a mile away. All he had to do was go to the end of this block then hang a left on Main and keep walking. He tried calling Tamarind again but got no signal.

People were calling out to each other as he walked. One guy looked at him. "You okay? Do you need a ride somewhere?"

Rick shook his head. "No, I'm fine. Heading just up the street here. But thanks."

As he walked, he had to step around devastation that he also tried to put out of his mind. One home looked pristine, with only a few branches in the yard. Its neighbor had the roof peeled back as if a giant wanted to explore the house.

*Oh, God, please...help these people.*

He stopped himself. Praying. It had rubbed off on him. Listening to Tamarind and watching her, spending time with Herb and the others at the up-at-the-crack-of-stupid study every week. Of course it had. They prayed, talked about God as if He was concerned about their lives, and they tried to help others in the community. They'd taken him as he was, questions and all. If it was all a divine sort of delusion, he wasn't sure it was a bad thing.

What if it wasn't a delusion? What if it—no, He—was real? In spite of everything he'd seen over the years?

Rick quickened his steps. Not far now. Millicent House had glistened at its opening. What would he find now? Did his insurance policy cover things like tornadoes? Of course, this was tornado alley, but he hadn't really thought about that fact.

Until now.

The streets were eerily deserted. Sirens wailed in

the distance. Rick thought of Herb. *God, Herb is one of the good guys. He sacrificed himself for me…for me. Please, give him a chance.*

Rick gritted his teeth as he took a few jogging steps. Then he limped back to a walk. He'd hit the concrete of the drainage pipe with more force than he realized. Of course, when you were being propelled by a wiry, muscular old veteran, whatever you came into contact with would hurt.

He reached the front sidewalk that led up to the double doors of Millicent House. Then when he saw the building itself, he sank down on one knee. Yes, it was a cruel joke from the Almighty. Rick bragging about owning a place that would surpass Tamarind's little café. Of course God was on Tamarind's side, if there were sides to be taken.

His phone rang. *Tamarind.* "Yeah."

"Rick, where are you?"

"I just got to Millicent House."

"And? How is it?"

"Part of the roof is torn off the dining room area. I haven't even looked inside yet."

"The power's out."

"Yes."

"I'm at The Pit. Dad's rigged up a generator to save what we've got in the walk-in. If you want, I can send him down there with his truck to help you clear out yours."

*The food.* He hadn't thought of that. They didn't open until suppertime during the week, so thankfully no one had been at his restaurant. But the food. It wouldn't keep. And the last thing on people's minds right now would be dining on elk barbecue.

"Yes, yes. That would be great." But the call had been dropped.

Five minutes later, Cleo Brown arrived in his large red pickup truck. "Hey, Rick. Praise God you're all right."

"Yes, Mr. Brown, I'm fine. I appreciate you coming down here. I don't want this food going bad, especially if we don't know when power's going to be back on." He motioned toward the parking lot. "Follow me around back, and I'll open up."

Rick unlocked the back door of the restaurant. Ironic, especially since the lack of a roof left the front of the building exposed. He entered the delivery area and pulled open the walk-in refrigerator. The temperature was already rising.

"Take all the meat," he said as Cleo entered the refrigerator. "Produce, too."

"They say the twister cut a mile strip crossways through town." Cleo shook his head. "Did you see it?"

"I saw it." Rick yanked a box of briskets from the shelf and placed them on the dolly Cleo held.

"Powerful stuff, these storms. I've lived here over twenty years, never seen anything this bad in our area. There was the Jarrell tornado about fifty miles from here in 1997. An EF5."

Rick continued piling the rest of his stock onto the dolly. "What was this one?"

"Judging by the damage, maybe an EF3 or a mild EF4. But I'm no expert. We're going to have a lot of people looking for help. I was up on the hill…saw it go through. First thought was of my baby girl, down here in town." Cleo's tone had a tightness to it, as if he forced the words out one syllable at a time as they squeezed through his vocal cords.

"I know." Rick only managed those two words.

"My children are my treasures. I don't care how old they get. And she's our baby. Can't help but see that little girl, runnin' after me, always wanting to know everything about everything." Cleo pulled back on the stocked dolly. "I don't want anything, or anyone, to hurt her. 'Cause she's been hurt before."

"I would never want to hurt her. That's why…" Rick paused. "That's why I've backed off, given her space. I know we're from two different places. Hers is here. My place is here for now…. Plus, there's the whole religion thing. I respect her decision." He thought of the "nondate" at Rebecca's and how they both danced close to that line.

"Son, I know." Cleo let the dolly sit upright and closed the space between them to grip Rick's shoulder. "My wife shouldn't have done what she did. Not an honest or a Christian thing to do, changing that card on the flowers. Tamarind deserved to know who truly sent them, and not in the way it panned out."

"Well, it would have been nice to hear that from your wife." The words came out a little more sharply than he'd intended. "I'm sorry, but Tamarind is an adult woman, capable of making her own decisions. I know she still lives at home with you all, but I hope your wife understands that Tamarind's not six, or even sixteen, anymore."

"You're right. I know. Hard thing, to let someone

go." Cleo nodded. "We ought to get this food over to The Pit. I have a feeling there will be a lot of hungry people tonight."

The street in front of The Pit was full of traffic, with some people arriving on foot. Starlight Fire Department across the street was empty, with all personnel out on the road. Tamarind took her handwritten poster-board sign and the tape outside.

Free Hot Meals Tonight, the sign proclaimed. It was the least she could do. Mom and Dad had met her at the restaurant. She'd almost cried when she saw the place intact, with only a few small twigs in the parking lot. A few diehards from the regular lunch crowd wanted to stay, offering to help.

"Please, make sure your homes and families are all right first," she'd told them. Her thoughts were of Azalea and Herb at Scott & White Hospital, forty miles away. Azalea had called once to say they were doing CAT scans and eventually surgery, but she wasn't sure what kind just yet. He had leg fractures, a punctured lung. They didn't know what else.

Her father's truck roared into the front parking lot, with Rick riding shotgun and the truck bed heaped with boxes and mesh bags of produce. Tamarind turned to face the glass door and tacked the sign to the glass.

Her heart had leaped with relief at Rick's call then dashed to the ground in anguish. He was out of the truck in a few seconds and stood beside her.

"I'm glad you're okay." He touched her hair, and she remembered again how the frizzies had attacked it.

"Yes. But you have a cut on your head. You should

get that looked at." She allowed herself to touch his forehead before clutching the adhesive tape with both hands.

"I...I didn't know." He studied her face. "You look
like you've been out in the rain."

"The roof blew off Chin Mae's salon." She moved
around him, stepping toward her father's truck. "Thanks
for bringing your food down here. It's going to be a
busy afternoon."

"I can see that. Free hot meals tonight? Then we
should probably get to work." He joined her at the truck.
"I brought my case of knives. We need to get this un-
loaded."

"Make yourself at home." She allowed herself a
smile. "We might have a crew showing up to help us.
I sent my workers home to check on their family and
friends and to let their neighborhoods know about the
meals tonight."

He flashed his own smile at her. "We'll get everything put together."

Tamarind lost the afternoon in a blur of cooking
prep. Her mother had bristled at the sight of Rick at the
restaurant, but Tamarind solved that sticky situation by
asking her to see if any stores would be willing to sell
or donate drinks for diners tonight.

Working with Rick in the kitchen was an unfamil-
iar dance. They'd never cooked together before, but she
found she liked his high energy, even if he was a bit
frenetic with his knife work. He could slice a pile of onions better than she could, so she stuck to slicing beef.

"There's no time to smoke any of this meat," she ob-
served as she looked at the elk steaks. "Do you want to

just keep this in the walk-in until we need it? Elk isn't cheap. We can grill it if you'd like."

"I was hoping to give some free samples for Millicent House, so why not now?" Rick shrugged. "We can grill those at the last minute if you slice them into six-ounce fillets now."

"I can't believe you're using this situation as a promotion for your business." Tamarind shook her head. "You know that's what some people will think."

Rick swung to face her, a look of shock on his face. "That's not what I meant. This is a gift. I'm not going to gain anything from this financially. If anything, I'm losing money. I have a restaurant that's missing part of its roof. Anyway, someone could say the same about you, the darling of Starlight or not."

She crossed her arms over her chest. "I'm not doing this for myself. I'm trying to make the most of a bad situation." *Darling of Starlight?* She paused. "Do you think some people believe that of me?"

"Some people will always believe the worst, even if your intentions are the best." Rick shrugged. "Sorry. I didn't mean to sound like I'm trying to promote myself here. I just find it ironic."

"I guess it is, now that you mention it." The Darling of Starlight… She wasn't…or was she? She didn't try to push herself to the front of situations. Her mother had dragged her into emceeing for the sweetheart night. But she'd liked the moment of being glammed up, in spite of the tortuous heels. She liked controlling the flow of the evening after all. Tamarind tried not to sigh. Despite Rick's sarcasm—she linked it to the high emotions of the day—she found a grain of truth inside the remark.

They went back to cooking and prep, but she realized how much she enjoyed working with him, and how much she'd missed him. The distance between them was for the best. They could talk and laugh about work, and right now, figure out how to be there for people. Then once the cleanup was done, Rick could go on his merry way.

"Schatze, there's someone here from the news," her mother called into the kitchen.

"News?"

Her mother rounded the corner to the cooking line. "Television. They want to talk to you. I saw the reporter at the firehouse, and I told her what you were doing."

"Doing?" Tamarind managed to parrot back. News? Here? At The Pit? "But I don't know what to say."

"Go ahead, you'll do fine," Rick said as he sliced a freshly smoked beef brisket. "This is a good opportunity for you, to show how people take care of each other around here."

"I agree with Rick here." Her mother nodded. "Go, freshen up. The customers won't be here for another hour at least."

"Freshen up. Ha." But Tamarind shook her head and went to her office. She would have preferred a fresh change of clothes, after getting rained on. Her jeans were still soaked from the ankles down, her T-shirt smudged from stopping to pull a tree out of the road. At least she found a wide hair band to pull her hair back.

In thirty seconds, she was standing in front of The Pit, facing a camera and a well-coiffed reporter. *Darling of Starlight, huh?*

"Caitlin Reynolds, Channel 11, Waco, the Killeen bureau." The blond shook Tamarind's hand. "We're going live in a minute or so for an update from here in Starlight, so when we're shooting, just look at me if you're not sure what to do."

"Okay."

"Your mother filled me in on what you're doing, and my boss at the home office said to cover it." Caitlin flexed her fingers as she held the microphone. "Counting down..." The camera operator counted back from five, folding down one finger on his right hand as he held the camera propped on his shoulder with the other.

"Caitlin Reynolds, live here in Starlight where an EF3 tornado touched down and wreaked a path of destruction one mile wide that cut the town in half." She blinked and paused. "At this time, there are some casualties but no reported fatalities as a result of the storm. Much of the town is without power.

"I'm standing here with Tamarind Brown, owner and operator of The Pit Barbecue and More. Tamarind, could you tell us where you were when the twister touched down?"

"Well, uh, Caitlin, I was at a nail salon not too far from here, getting ready to have a pedicure with my best friend. We knew a storm was going to hit, but that's not a surprise, here in Texas. Then the four of us heard the siren and took shelter in a bathroom. The salon lost its roof, and some vehicles were moved around. Nobody was hurt where we were, that I know of." *Breathe, breathe. You're talking too fast.* The memory of hours before swirled around and tightened in her throat.

"Tamarind and her parents were fortunate in that their home was unharmed by the storm. However, they know that their friends and neighbors haven't fared as well. That's why Tamarind is opening her restaurant tonight, and they have power with the aid of a generator. Can you tell us more about your plans?"

The microphone swung her way again. "We're opening for dinner tonight—for free. A lot of people have food that won't keep or have lost what they have. So anyone who needs a meal, come on by. We have good brisket and pork sandwiches. Burgers, too. Plus one of the other restaurants in town is joining with me. Chef Rick Mantovani, owner of Millicent House, lost part of his dining room roof today. He's in my kitchen now, working on dinner prep." She hoped she wasn't babbling.

Caitlin faced the camera. "The local Red Cross is also on hand to help, and local city fire and public safety workers are ensuring that Starlight's citizens are safe." She swung to face Tamarind once again. "I understand a good family friend of yours was seriously injured today."

"Um, yes. Herb Bush. He's like an uncle to a lot of us in town. He was injured by debris while trying to help someone to safety. He's at Scott & White in Temple now. Looking at surgery. I pray he'll be all right." Tamarind's eyes burned, and she blinked. This was a million times worse than emceeing the Starlight and Sweethearts gala.

"We hope so, too, Tamarind. Back to you at the studio, Jim. We'll give you another update at the 6 p.m. broadcast." The light on the camera dimmed, and Caitlin looked at Tamarind. "That was great. We might stop by later for an update, if that's okay."

"Yes, sure." *Hold it together for a few more minutes, girl.*

"We'll see you then."

Tamarind nodded and watched them leave then fled to the familiar surroundings of the restaurant. Pulse pounding, she entered the kitchen as Rick looked up.

"You okay?" he asked. "How'd it go? Get tongue-tied at all?"

"No, I didn't." She spoke around her breaths. "I'll be right back." She passed the office doorway and rounded the corner to the smoking pit. She entered the semi-darkness and inhaled the scent of mesquite, the warm woody aroma engulfing her. She pulled back the grill cover. A pair of briskets were about ready to come off the grill top. Who'd have thought eighteen hours ago, as she laid the freshly seasoned cuts of meat over the smoky flame, how much things could change?

She heard footsteps and turned to see Rick enter the pit. "These are about ready to come off."

He pulled her close. "Are you sure you're all right?"

She crumbled. "Rick, it was awful. I've lived here almost my whole life but never seen anything like this happen before. And Uncle Herb..." She allowed herself one sob on Rick's shoulder. "I know God's going to take care of him, but it's hard knowing that people I care about were in trouble today. I'm trying to be strong."

"And you are.... You went right out there and talked to that reporter, you decided to open The Pit tonight and give food away. You're amazing, Tamarind Brown. You inspire me." He planted a kiss on the top of her head.

"Oh, Rick." She lifted her face to him and allowed

herself to meet his eyes. He didn't move toward her, but she could feel his intensity.

A kiss would have to be her choice. She'd have to be the one to step over that invisible line she'd helped draw between them. She wanted to kiss him, wanted to hop on the roller coaster and race downhill, with more G-force than the Titan at Six Flags, feeling weightless in his embrace as everything else went silent. But then she'd want more, more than she or he had a right to at this time. Not another heat-of-the-moment kiss.

She reached up and caressed his face instead.

## Chapter 16

"You do inspire me." Rick felt his throat stick. "Today's been horrible. But something Herb said got me thinking about a lot of things. I...uh... I even prayed for him today. I don't know if God listened." He wasn't sure how to explain it and felt his face flush.

"That's good. I...I know you've been going to the Bible study now and again."

"Yeah, well, Herb can be pretty persuasive." Tamarind laughed for the first time today. "I hope Azalea calls soon."

"We'll see how those prayers are working, if God's going to do it." Tamarind leaned her head on his shoulder. "Just because we don't always get the answer we want doesn't mean God's not doing something. He's much more than a good-luck charm."

"I didn't mean that. I just meant if we pray, then *something* should happen. Of course, I prayed when I was a kid, but we had to make sure we prayed enough." He tried to find the right words. "Part of me really wants to believe. I do. But then…" He realized he still held her in his arms, and he released her.

"What did Herb say that made you think?"

"He said something like, 'The Lord isn't in the wind—listen for His still, small voice.' Do you have any idea what that means?"

Tamarind nodded. "There's a story in the Bible about the prophet Elijah, who was told to wait because the Lord was going to pass by him. He hid in a crack in the mountain, and first came the wind, then an earthquake, then a fire. But the Lord wasn't in any of those. When the Lord came to Elijah, he listened for the still, small voice, and then the Lord called Elijah out from his hiding place to see Him."

"So what does Herb mean by that? Why did he say that to me?" Both Herb and Tamarind knew something he didn't, as if the meaning should be obvious. But it wasn't, at least not to him.

"I'm not a hundred percent sure. Maybe he doesn't want you to blame God for what happened today. Maybe if…if you're searching for answers, you need to be still and listen." She shrugged. "I…I don't know."

"I know I don't understand why this happened today. Maybe Herb doesn't want me to blame God, but I do know that God let it happen. If God is supposed to love us—love Herb—then why is Herb fighting for his life right now?" Rick tried not to raise his voice, but he couldn't help the tone. This was one thing he never understood about religious people. The idea of prayer, the idea of doing good, the idea of bettering oneself.

He understood that. But how they could just smile and nod that "God's will" was being worked out when the most unfair things happened? He didn't get it.

"I'm not sure why God let this happen. I would love to know." Tamarind's voice shook. "Sometimes we don't get all the answers."

"That's a very convenient answer for right now." Rick took a step back. "Look, I know we have dinner prep and a crowd that's going to show up now that the word is out about free dinner. We should get busy."

"You're right. We should." Tamarind sighed and glanced at the brisket on the grill. "I'll be right in."

Stubborn man. But good questions about something she couldn't explain herself. She knew in her heart that Herb was in God's hands. But being in God's hands didn't mean that bad things didn't happen. She realized she'd had it pretty easy her whole life. Her father had faced danger in his military career but emerged unscathed. Her brother and sisters were healthy, safe. The idea of something happening, though, to someone she loved...

She took an empty sheet pan from the prep table beside the smoker and found herself questioning, much as Rick had. *Why, God?* She didn't want to ask why. In the end, there weren't always answers. But she did know certain things. Nothing could separate her from God's love—not even death or the pain that it caused. The Bible told her that, and she'd learned the verses from Romans when she was a child.

Had she always loved God because her life was easy? What if it wasn't? She'd been coddled like a sweetheart all her life. The thought of anything bad happening frightened her.

No wonder Mary and Martha had chided Jesus. *"Lord, if You'd been here, our brother wouldn't have died."* If only, if only. Now one of the sweetest, biggest hearts she'd ever known lay at death's door. Herb Bush wasn't a young man physically. But now shouldn't be his time to go. This worry was far, far worse than her restaurant losing money, and Mike stealing from her, and that broken trust.

Her father burst into the smoker pit with Rick on his heels. "We just heard from Azalea." Her father's voice cracked. "Herb's gone."

Tamarind clamped her hand over her mouth to stifle her sob. Rick put his arms around her. "No, no, no…"

Rick nodded to her father. "I'll stay with her."

Herb couldn't be gone. He was the one who told her all the goofy jokes and had taken to playing video games like a teenager. He was the one who'd come to everyone's rescue with his tow truck at least once. His faith, solid as the rocks pulled from the quarries in the hill country, had inspired many in Starlight.

She pulled away from Rick, wiping tears from her face. "There's no time for this now. Herb would be telling us we have a lot of people to feed, people who need us."

"He probably would." Rick blinked in rapid succession, probably not from the smoke. "A lot of good prayer did. A lot of good anything did."

"Don't say that." But she realized the same statement echoed in her heart. What good had their prayers done?

Somehow they pushed through and served nearly two

hundred people who came through. They sent wrapped sandwiches across the street to the fire department. Tamarind couldn't imagine the tough job they faced, going through debris, accounting for everyone. So far, no reported fatalities...besides Herb.

She sat down in the office and wiggled her sore feet after cleanup. They should preserve what fuel they had in the generator, but she was too numb after the day's events to worry about that. All she could think about was Azalea, for the first time in decades...alone.

Two figures appeared in the doorway. Liann and Justine. "You heard about Uncle Herb?"

Tamarind nodded, and her tears came again. The three women made a group hug. "I can't believe it," Tamarind mumbled. "It wasn't supposed to be this way."

Liann sniffled. "No. What will Starlight do without him?"

Justine reached for a tissue. "What will Aunt Zalea do without him?"

"They were always spitting and sputtering about this or that," Tamarind said. "They'd come in for breakfast some days and stay till almost lunchtime, drinking coffee." The thought made her laugh.

"We need to do something for Aunt Zalea." Justine stepped back and leaned against the office wall.

"It's early, though." Liann sat down on the empty chair across from Tamarind's desk. "There's so much going on now, with the cleanup and all. Aunt Chin Mae is with her."

"Good. It's important to have your best friends nearby at times like this." Justine nodded. "Oh, girls, it just doesn't seem real."

Tamarind grabbed the box of tissues and passed it to the other women. "No. I want to wake up from this, but I can't."

Dad appeared in the office doorway. "Has anyone seen Rick? He's disappeared."

# Chapter 17

Tamarind never realized that a person can experience all the emotions of a lifetime in the space of a week. She felt like her heart had been removed from her chest, kicked around the room, then tucked back inside her again without so much as a thank-you.

Her phone remained silent, except for her parents touching base with her, or Liann or Justine, especially with preparations for the after-funeral meal.

But no Rick. She'd left him a message without a return call. The one time she stopped by Millicent House, his manager, a guy named Franco, said that Rick was busy, making preparations to fly back to New Jersey.

Tamarind's own heartbreak, she knew, was nothing like what Azalea was going through. Herb Bush, like so many other Vietnam veterans, had lived out his life quietly and battled his demons. But in doing so, he touched the lives of everyone he met. Or so said Pastor

Mark in comforting words that left them bawling like so many babies as Herb's body was laid to rest at the Central Texas Veterans' Cemetery.

Today's sunny blue sky was a poor apology for the tornado just over one week ago. Power was restored to town, and most of the debris had been trucked away. Only scarred buildings remained, and scarred memories. People still banded together, especially those with homes or businesses damaged by the storm. It somehow made personal griefs easier to carry. People didn't feel so alone that way.

Tamarind walked along, zigzagging along Starlight's streets to the quaint older neighborhood where the Bushes kept their simple ranch-style home, built more than forty years before. Maybe Aunt Azalea didn't want company. She had enough food to feed an elementary school, likely, after the funeral. She who had made more casseroles in the last several decades than just about anyone else in Starlight now found herself on the receiving end of blessing and comfort.

The irony made Tamarind smile, just a bit, as she stood at the Bushes' front door. This was a bad idea. If she were in Azalea's place, she'd want to be left alone. But then, she'd never been in a situation like this herself. She knocked.

Azalea opened the door. "Why Tamarind, I didn't hear a car drive up." She glanced up and down the street.

"No. I walked."

"You *walked*?" Azalea shook her head. "Get in here, young lady. Your skinny little legs are probably ready to fall off. That, and you need some sweet tea."

Skinny and little weren't adjectives usually used to

describe Tamarind's legs, and she almost giggled at the words. Not that her legs were big, but they certainly weren't skinny.

"Okay," she said as Azalea pulled her inside.

"C'mon in the kitchen, dear." Azalea led the way to a sprawling farmhouse-style kitchen. Nice. Tamarind was impressed with the large space. The couple had likely redone it at some point, as none of the retro appliances or finishes existed in the space.

Tamarind perched at the breakfast bar while Azalea rummaged in the stainless fridge. "Sakes alive, I'm going to have to have a dinner party or something. Too much food. Guess it's payback." She pulled out a jug of tea.

"Rick is gone, and he hasn't come back," was all Tamarind could think of to say. "I knew he was going to leave, but the storm..." As if Rick going were the biggest issue any of them were facing.

"I know what happened." Azalea set a glass of tea in front of Tamarind. "Herb woke up long enough in the hospital that day to tell me. He... He wanted to make sure young Rick was okay. He was as fond of him... as fond of..." She gulped and reached for a dish towel, holding it up to her eyes.

"I know.... Rick thought the world of Herb, he did." Tamarind's eyes brimmed with tears, and she brushed them away. She was tired of crying. Didn't cry as a rule, but during the last week she'd more than made up for it.

"I've done soaked through all these towels." Azalea wiped her eyes. "I was tryin' to say, Herb was as fond of young Rick as he would have been one of his own sons.

Times like now, makes me wish we'd at least adopted a few kids, since we couldn't have any of our own."

"You have all of us, Aunt Azalea." Blah. She was sniffling again.

"I know, I know. We always had our Starlight kids. I just never imagined how life would be without my Herb." She shook her head.

"Well, I was thinking about you and wanted to come by. But I didn't know what to say."

"Just you bein' here is wonderful. You always took such good care of me and Herb from your kitchen, I'm happy to do the same for you here in mine." Azalea studied Tamarind's face. "I'm not…I'm not sure what to do now, Tamarind."

"But that's okay, right now. You be good to yourself," Tamarind said.

"That sounds like something my Herb would have said. 'You're always fussin' over someone else; you need to be good to yourself sometimes, too,' he'd say." Azalea sighed. "Maybe I'll start by taking swimming lessons."

"Swimming lessons?"

"I can go on post and do that. I still have military privileges, being retired."

Tamarind stared at the older woman. "That's a good idea."

"Herb would never go. He'd harp about getting in the water with complete strangers." Azalea chuckled at the memory. "Oh, my. I have no idea how people without Jesus manage grief. I surely don't. I miss him so, but my Herb knew exactly where he was going, and he was ready. One thing he always wanted to be sure of, that he was ready to go."

"Yes, that he was."

"We'll just be prayin' for that young man of yours. I know he's not quite sure what to do about Jesus yet. So that's why this has been so awful for him." Azalea patted Tamarind's hand.

"It probably has." Tamarind nodded. Here she'd gone to see Azalea to comfort her somehow, and Azalea turned her grief around, as deep as it was, and turned to face what Rick must be going through.

*Oh, Rick...*

He was a coward, and he didn't blame the entire population of Starlight if they hated him for robbing them of their beloved Herb Bush. Rick stared out into the alley behind Pasta-Pasta, listening to the sounds of the city at night. Millicent House was running smoothly in the hands of Franco and Matt, and Rick wouldn't need to stay in Texas long the next time he traveled south. He couldn't see closing the restaurant once the roof was fixed. He owed the town that much, to keep the business open. Who knows? Maybe one of them, even Matt, would buy it at cost, so Rick would at least break even with the whole sorry mess.

He should have known that following the trail of his heart down to Texas and Tamarind Brown would end badly. She'd been right. They had so much in common, amazing chemistry, and enjoyed being together in so many ways—except in the one area that counted most, especially to her.

When the bottom caved out of the world, people wanted someone who shared the same core beliefs. Right now he didn't think he believed what Tamarind did. Especially after losing Herb. It was his fault. He should have tried harder, fought the older man's stubbornness and forced him into that ditch. And God, in the sick irony that the heavens had wrought on Starlight that day, yanked Herb away from this earth too soon.

*It should not have ended like this.*

"Rick." A hand rested on his shoulder. "You need a breather, Chef?"

Julio, his executive chef, stood beside him. "I've been calling you, Chef. If you need a break, we got it here. Come back at closing, no?"

"A breather."

"Go for a walk. You're no good to me here, as you'd say."

He almost wanted to laugh. "Using my own words against me? Now I can't argue with that. I'll be back later."

Rick stepped out the back of the restaurant into the cool air. The evening still had a bite in it, a little cooler than Texas. But he unbuttoned his chef jacket anyway as he strolled the alley. Steam rose from vents, and the streets were still slick with rain that had fallen earlier that day.

He headed onto the sidewalk, surprisingly empty for an evening. Sunday. That's what day it was. He almost couldn't remember. Had he been back here a week or more? He couldn't remember that either. Rick walked, not counting the blocks as he did so but instead kept up an inner tirade that propelled him along:

*How can I believe in a God that will let me down? This isn't asking for help with a business. Or something for myself. If God let Herb Bush die, then He could and probably would do the same to Dad. Or anyone. Russian roulette at its finest. Pull the trigger—oh, goody! You lucked out.*

"I don't like this deal, God," he said aloud, not caring who saw him. "I have to stay away from sin, but You can't do me the favor of keeping my friends alive, or safe? Then, I don't love Tamarind Brown, either. If I don't love her, then You can't take her from me." Trouble was, he did love Tamarind Brown, as much as he loved breathing. No, more than that. The idea of living in this world, without her in it…

Organ music snapped him out of his musings. He looked up. Half a block ahead, a neon sign lit up the darkness—Starlight Gospel Mission. Now that was ironic. And cruel.

Rick glared up at the cloudy night. "Very funny, God." But he let his feet carry him toward the open doors.

"I am the resurrection and the life…" A loud voice boomed from a speaker, and the organ echoed. "He who believes in me, though he were dead… Yet. Shall. He. Live!"

Rick stopped in the doorway in time to see a congregation leap to their feet, shouting. "Glory to God! Amen!" The words of the preacher made him pause.

He remembered those words, in the largest book of John…. One of Jesus' friends had died, one of his good friends….

The minister reminded Rick of Cleo Brown in posture, tone, and voice. He held up his Bible and said, "Let me read this again in case you need to hear it again. We all need to hear it again…from the eleventh chapter of the book of John. 'Lord,' Martha said to Jesus, 'if you had been here, my brother would not have died. But I know that even now God will give you whatever you ask.' Jesus said to her, 'Your brother will rise again.' Martha answered, 'I know he will rise again in the resurrection at the last day.' Jesus said to her, 'I am the resurrection and the life. The one who believes in me will live, even though they die; and whoever lives by believing in me will never die. Do you believe this?'

"So my question to you, my brothers and sisters, is: Do you believe this?"

*I don't know.* Rick slipped inside the chapel and found an empty spot on a wooden pew. He was still angry, but the words he'd read in the Bible came back to him.

"Either we believe Jesus is who He says He is, or it's all a lie and nothing. If we do not believe, it is for *nothing.*"

The minister continued, "We must all decide for ourselves. Either God is God, and Jesus is our Savior, or not. We can't have it both ways. We can't live like we want to and disregard what Jesus did for us—to give us that life, redemption, hope. We can't treat our heavenly Father like a genie in a bottle, because He's not.

"I don't know what you all have faced in this life, but I do know this—God is who He says He is, regardless of what happens to us. He does not change, and He alone is the anchor we cling to."

Rick glanced around the small, modest chapel. This was a homeless shelter. Men in varying types of clothing dotted the pews. The preacher was likely a guest, as was the woman at the organ and a few dressed-up people on the front seats.

"And now, I invite you to come forward tonight if you need prayer. I thank Brother Zeke for having us as guests tonight. Brother Zeke."

To Rick's surprise, a young Caucasian man about his age stepped forward. "Thank you, Reverend Williams, for that strong and uplifting word tonight. Let's pray before we dismiss. We have supper ready in the back for those of you who haven't eaten, but don't pass up the opportunity for prayer if you need it."

Rick bowed his head. He wasn't sure if he was going to pray or what he would say if he did. *God, please, be real to me. Because it hurts right now. I'm so angry about Herb. If Jesus is the resurrection and the life, then Herb is okay. Because I know he believed in You.*

"Would you like to go forward, young man?" The preacher stood at his end of the pew.

"I…I think I would."

A few others had stepped forward. On numb legs, Rick went to the front of the chapel and bowed his head. *Lord, forgive me, for I have sinned. It has been many years since my last confession. God, that's all I know to do. But reading the book of John tells me that You love me…. I'm Your son. Please, forgive me.*

Two strong hands rested on Rick's shoulders. "Oh Lord, You know that grief is great. Your own Son, the man of sorrows, is acquainted with grief. Bear my brother's burden, restore his joy. Better than that, give him a joy and assurance such that he has never known before. We are worth far, far more than sparrows that fall. You see the sparrow fall, and You see us. We can say, like Job, 'I know my redeemer lives, and that after my flesh be destroyed, yet shall I see God.' We ourselves will see Him."

Rick heard himself wail, and powerful arms surrounded him. "Lord, give my brother Your peace."

He felt like he'd just come home.

# Chapter 18

"It's been weeks now." Tamarind sighed. "And it all feels just wrong." Chin Mae's roof was repaired, and she had invited everyone to come down for a free manicure or pedicure. Tamarind, Liann, and Justine sat in a row, soaking their feet.

"He still won't answer your calls?" Liann asked.

"I stopped calling. I'm no stalker." At that, the other women laughed, and Tamarind managed a smile.

The bell jingled over the door. "Is this where I can get a pedicure?"

"Aunt Zalea!" Justine called out.

"You come right in," Chin Mae said. "These girls clog up the chairs, so you have to wait. Manicure?"

"Well sure, why not?" Azalea plopped herself onto the nearest cushioned manicure chair. "I've been nibbling my nails down to nubs anyhow. I figure if my best friend's business is open again, the least I can do is help her out."

"Oh, Azalea, you're too funny." Chin Mae sat down across from her friend. "You need to stop chewing. It's not good for you."

Azalea glanced over to Tamarind and the others. "Hello, my favorite three nieces."

They waved. Tamarind recalled the visit she'd paid Azalea, not long after Uncle Herb's funeral. She'd seen Azalea only at church since.

"So, Miss Brown?" asked Azalea.

"Yes, ma'am?"

"Have you heard from that young man of yours?"

"No, I haven't."

Azalea made a clucking noise. "You need to go after him. Make a stand for him. Because—ow, Chin Mae. That's the quick of my fingernails you're poking."

"Stop complaining and let me work. It's no worse than what you've done to them." Chin Mae shook her head.

"As I was saying… Go after him. Go to New York. If he turns you away, at least you know. Because life is too…too short." At that, Azalea's voice caught.

The older woman's chiding made tears come to Tamarind's eyes. She'd told herself to hold back, to not pursue a man. Rightly so. But with Rick, it was different. She couldn't leave things in limbo like this. Maybe he could, but she couldn't.

"I hear the shopping is really good in New York," Tamarind said.

"Oh, I wish school was out. I'd go with you," Liann offered. "Unless you want to go on a weekend?"

"Y'all...I think...I think I'd rather go by myself." Tamarind wasn't sure if it was the best idea. She'd never flown before. The biggest city she'd been to was Houston, and only to a suburb.

Before she changed her mind, as soon as the pedicure was over, she booked a flight to New York. How to find him, though? She wasn't sure the manager of Millicent House would give her his home address or his parents' address. Well, she could show up at his restaurants. If she was a customer, he couldn't turn her away. Not exactly.

Rick sat in his favorite corner of the dining room at Mantovani's. The peace and quiet of the late morning had given way to the first trickle of lunch customers. However, the peace and quiet had been first interrupted by a somewhat uncomfortable telephone call—a call that still had him immersed on the phone.

"Don't let your pride get in the way, Rick." Zeke's voice held wisdom beyond his years. The young minister had become a mentor to Rick ever since the night he'd stumbled upon Starlight Gospel Mission. He'd walked more than twelve blocks, he realized, from Pasta-Pasta. Since that night, he'd started volunteering. That is, until his father ended up back in the hospital with bypass surgery.

At last, Rick managed to respond. "I know. I left... not in a very good way. I was angry, bitter. Mad at the world and God. And now, enough time has gone by that I'm not sure what'll happen. I do need to get down to Texas again."

"It sounds like you have some good friends down there, though. They'll forgive you."

"But I hurt someone...someone I love." What Tamarind must think of him now...

"If she's that special, give her some credit. Even my wife and I have hurt each other, but we've always tried to give each other grace."

"Grace?" The churchy words, as he called them, still tripped him up.

"Not demanding the other 'pay' for what they've done. I bet she'll do that for you."

"I imagine she would."

"I know you're about to start your day over there. But I wanted to say thanks for donating food for our pantry and giving that cooking demo. It's been a big help. One of our regulars said something about maybe going to culinary school one day."

"That's awesome, Zeke. And you're very welcome. We'll see you this weekend."

"Super. Tell your mother I'm hoping for more of that manicotti."

"Done." He chuckled as they ended the call. His gaze traveled across the dining room, its classic decor giving the space an elegant atmosphere. There, in the doorway by the host's reception desk. *Tamarind?*

She stood there, tall and elegant in dark denim jeans topped with a white blouse and a red tailored jacket. One of her hands fumbled with a series of bracelets on the opposite wrist. She glanced around as she spoke to Luis, his maître d'.

Luis murmured something then gestured toward the corner where Rick now stood.

Tamarind crossed the dining room, leaving several appreciative glances behind her. Tamarind Brown? Here, in New York? At his restaurant?

At last she reached his table. "You left, without saying anything," was how she greeted him. "I just couldn't let you do that."

He cleared his throat and tried not to stammer. "You're right. Look, I…I'm sorry. So much has happened in the last few weeks." He took her by the hand and pulled her into the booth to sit down next to him. The story tumbled out. He wasn't sure he got it all in the right order, but when he was done, Tamarind was smiling that electric smile in his direction. She loved him. She had to, if she came all this way. A lady, full of grace. But of course she had plenty of grace.

"Dad's doing better now, and truthfully, I was planning a trip to Starlight again soon. But I wasn't sure…"

"Sure of what?"

He didn't answer. Of course, now that she'd cornered him—not that he was complaining at the moment—he didn't know exactly what to say.

"Well, now that I've heard your story, I'm sure of this." Tamarind kissed him, almost making him forget where he was. He caught the scent of her perfume, the same stuff she'd worn when Cleo dragged them to the shooting range. He pulled her still closer. How he'd missed her.

When the kiss was over, Tamarind looked at him and said, "Azalea Bush said life is too short, that I should come after you and find out once and for all…. So?" The quaver in her voice touched him to the core.

"Tamarind Brown, Azalea is right. Life is too short.

And I love you. I've loved you, I think, since last summer. I love you even more now. But I never want you to feel like you're settling for me. I still have so much to learn." He caressed the beautiful tawny skin of her face as her green eyes sparkled. "I promise you this, though. I'm going to spend my life being the man you deserve, if you'll have me."

"I will. Because I have a lot to learn, myself."

"We can keep learning...together." With that, Rick kissed her again.

# *Epilogue*

*June sixteenth, one year later,*
*in Liberty State Park,*
*New Jersey*

Tamarind wanted to pinch herself as she peeked out of the limousine window. Liberty State Park lay just outside, and beyond it, the Manhattan skyline. The western edges of the buildings glowed in the twilight, and one by one, lights started twinkling on for the evening. Or, for her and Rick.

Under a magnificent live oak tree on the lush green lawn, they'd had a simple wedding ceremony on June first in Starlight's city park. Well, simple if you counted three hundred guests and her father working overtime to smoke enough brisket for the reception at the Starlight Civic Center. How they'd missed Herb, who'd have beamed with joy for both of them.

Starlight had healed, at last, from its wounds of the previous year. After the reception, she and Rick had disappeared for three whole days at a bed and breakfast with no Internet and no phone service. It had been a *very* long engagement. Now they were celebrating up north with Rick's family and friends who couldn't make the trip to Texas.

"You ready to run the northern gauntlet, wife of mine?" Rick asked.

"I sure am."

"Kevin's not so sure. He thinks you'll upset our balance in the business."

"Ha. Well, maybe one day we'll buy *him* out." She leaned over and kissed him. "But enough talk about business tonight. Is that kiss enough to tide you over until later?"

He pulled her close. "Until later... ?" He kissed her until she could scarcely breathe.

"Later," she managed to say. "We have a tent full of people and a ton of Italian food waiting for us. Fresh from Pasta-Pasta across the harbor."

"Killjoy." He pouted, and she kissed him again.

Liann rapped on the window outside. "It's time, y'all. Your public awaits." Liann and Justine had joined the party up north and had already filled two suitcases with treasures from some heavy-duty shopping trips.

Yes, it certainly was time. After tonight's northern reception, they'd be jetting off to Italy for their official honeymoon, to meet more of Rick's extended family. Tamarind had never been out of the country, hardly out of Texas.

After their honeymoon, they would return to New

York City. She'd grown to love it as she visited Rick's family and fallen in love with his parents as well. She enjoyed the vibrancy, the kaleidoscope of people, the restaurants as varied as those who dined inside. He'd proudly shown her Pasta-Pasta and his flagship restaurant, Mantovani's.

Now Millicent House and Tamarind's share of The Pit would slide alongside the others. The Pit would get its long-needed renovation, and Tamarind just might give Rick her top-secret barbecue recipe. They would make it work, living in New York and returning to Texas to see to their businesses there. Plus, he'd taken her by the Starlight Gospel Mission. Together they laughed at the name, and he introduced her to Zeke. They both looked forward to helping him whenever he needed food for the mission's guests.

Tamarind inhaled a deep breath as the driver opened their door. The whole wide world lay before her, with the man of her dreams beside her to explore it. Yet, she would always love Starlight. Their children— the thought thrilled her—would have the best of both worlds. The warmth of small-town Texas with its wide, open spaces to feed their imagination and dreams, and another urban world that she was still getting to know.

"Ready, Mrs. Mantovani?"

"Ready, Mr. Mantovani."

A cheer rose from the crowd underneath the tent as they approached.

Rick paused on the walkway. "Will you miss Starlight?"

"Of course I will." Tamarind looked across the harbor and up at the night sky. "But I can't wait to see what's to come."

As if in response, a single star glowed above the Empire State Building. Starlight shone here, too. So did God's presence. He'd brought them down this road, a longer journey than they'd expected, to such a beautiful destination. A breeze drifted off the harbor, touched Tamarind's cheek, and swirled the hem of her red party dress.

She grinned at Rick. "And for me, home is wherever we are, together."

\* \* \* \* \*

# REQUEST YOUR FREE BOOKS!

## 2 FREE CHRISTIAN NOVELS
## PLUS 2
## FREE
## MYSTERY GIFTS

**HEARTSONG PRESENTS**

---

**YES!** Please send me 2 Free Heartsong Presents novels and my 2 FREE mystery gifts (gifts are worth about $10). After receiving them, if I don't wish to receive any more books I can return the shipping statement marked "cancel." If I don't cancel, I will receive 4 brand-new novels every month and be billed just $4.24 per book. That's a savings of 20% off the cover price. It's quite a bargain! Shipping and handling is just 50¢ per book in the U.S.* I understand that accepting the 2 free books and gifts places me under no obligation to buy anything. I can always return a shipment and cancel at any time. Even if I never buy another book, the two free books and gifts are mine to keep forever.

159 HDN FT97

Name _____ (PLEASE PRINT) _____

Address _____ Apt. # _____

City _____ State _____ Zip _____

Signature (if under 18, a parent or guardian must sign)

### Mail to the **Reader Service:**
**IN U.S.A.:** P.O. Box 1867, Buffalo, NY 14240-1867

Not valid for current subscribers to Heartsong Presents books.

\* Terms and prices subject to change without notice. Prices do not include applicable taxes. Sales tax applicable in N.Y. This offer is limited to one order per household. All orders subject to credit approval. Credit or debit balances in a customer's account(s) may be offset by any other outstanding balance owed by or to the customer. Please allow 4 to 6 weeks for delivery. Offer available while quantities last. Offer valid only in the U.S.

---

**Your Privacy**—The Reader Service is committed to protecting your privacy. Our Privacy Policy is available online at www.ReaderService.com or upon request from the Reader Service.

We make a portion of our mailing list available to reputable third parties that offer products we believe may interest you. If you prefer that we not exchange your name with third parties, or if you wish to clarify or modify your communication preferences, please visit us at www.ReaderService.com/consumerschoice or write to us at Reader Service Preference Service, P.O. Box 9062, Buffalo, NY 14269. Include your complete name and address.